# The Sellout

Andrew Diamond

ISBN – Paperback: 978-1734139297
ISBN – Kindle: 979-8988872207

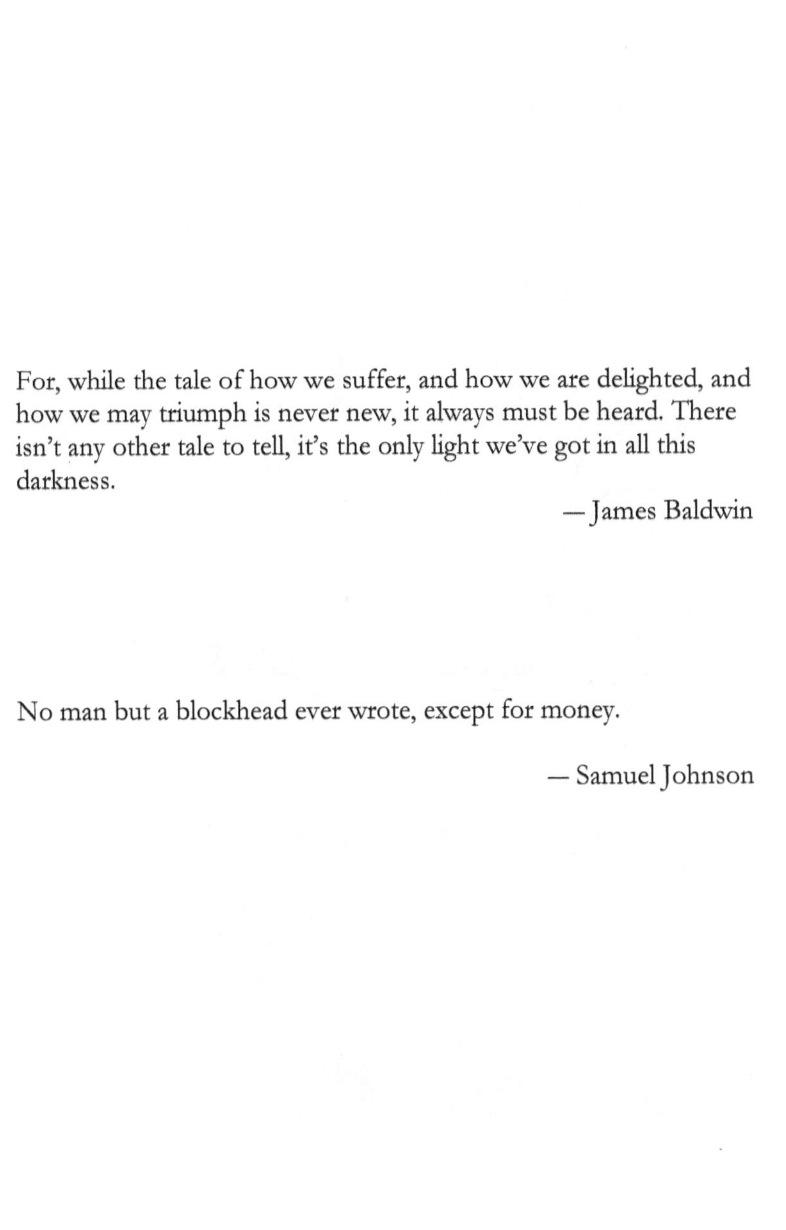

For, while the tale of how we suffer, and how we are delighted, and how we may triumph is never new, it always must be heard. There isn't any other tale to tell, it's the only light we've got in all this darkness.

— James Baldwin

No man but a blockhead ever wrote, except for money.

— Samuel Johnson

# Veronica's Curse

1

The first royalty check came in at just over sixty thousand. In less than six weeks, Joe McElwee's first thriller had earned back the advance and cracked the top ten of the *New York Times* bestseller list. His publisher hinted that the next check would top one hundred and fifty grand.

"And that's just the US trade and hardback market," his agent told him. "We haven't even gotten to foreign rights and streaming."

McElwee already had plans for the money. First, the car. Though he felt some affection for the twenty-three-year-old Chevy that had hauled him back and forth to adjunct professorships on a circuit of second-tier public universities, the Malibu had been wheezing blue smoke for the past twenty thousand miles. The seats were ripped, blotches of paint had faded and chipped from the hood and trunk, and the suspension was shot.

McElwee likened the car to an elderly dog: arthritic, hazy eyed, and deaf, but faithful to the last. He couldn't abandon it any more than he could have turned his back on a mutt who had stuck with him through his coldest, hungriest days.

Now that he could afford a new vehicle, he began to think differently. He told himself that even the greatest racehorses were eventually put out to pasture. It was the humane thing to do. Give the beast some rest.

When he tried to picture what "pasture" looked like for an old beaten-down sedan, the image of his abandoned Chevy rusting in a junkyard pained him. He forced his mind instead to the Mercedes dealership. He'd twice driven past without stopping. All those years of instant coffee breakfasts and rice-

and-bean dinners made him feel like a creature of a different species, an impostor who didn't belong in an upscale car dealership.

The other night, he dreamed he was in the showroom, asking the dealer about a sensible entry-level CLA-class sedan. The dealer smiled and whispered with a polite and knowing smile, "Why don't you make this easy on us both and just leave?" McElwee looked up to see another salesman shooing him out with a subtle hand gesture, the way the maître d' of a fine restaurant might discreetly rid his establishment of a homeless person who'd wandered in off the street.

The first check, the sixty thousand, had just cleared that morning. After years of living hand-to-mouth—the associate professorships were part-time gigs that paid near minimum wage—he had developed a fear of spending money. He had splurged and bought two new suits on credit before the check cleared, then kept them in the closet for two days, wrapped in plastic, in case he had to return them.

Now that the money was in his account, he felt safe to wear his new clothes. When he'd given readings in the past, he'd dressed like a man without money: jeans or khakis, always faded, and an ill-fitting button-down shirt because Goodwill and the Salvation Army didn't always carry his size. Beggars can't be choosers.

For today's reading, he chose the lighter of the two suits, a medium-blue, pure Merino wool costing more than a full month's rent. The first step in gaining the respect that had eluded him for all of his professional life, he told himself, was to look respectable.

A little voice inside his head said, "I don't buy that."

He told the voice to shut up.

The voice said, "If you want respect, *be* respectable. It's not something you put on. It's what you are inside, how you act in the world, how you treat others."

McElwee asked the voice if the guy on the Mercedes lot would respect him more in his Goodwill hand-me-downs or his sharp new suit.

Then came another thought, one that had nagged him earlier that morning as he dressed. Was a nine-hundred-dollar suit good enough? If he wanted to make a mark in the world, why had he skimped? Why not go for the two-thousand-dollar job?

Funny how money changes you, he thought. One day, I'm terrified at the extravagance of dropping nine hundred bucks on a new suit. The next day, it's not good enough.

Is this how rich people think, he wondered. Is this why they never think they have enough?

When the thought became uncomfortable, he dismissed it and turned his mind to the money to come. The publisher had signed him to a one-book deal. Obviously, they wanted to extend that now. After today's reading, he'd head to New York to meet with his agent and publisher.

The publisher wanted four more titles to follow *Extraordinary Joe*. The protagonist of McElwee's first thriller was the most popular element of his wildly popular book. Outwardly, everything about the character seemed ordinary. He was a man of no means with average looks, driving an average car. He'd learned to fight in Afghanistan, where he developed the PTSD that made him hide from the world, keep a low-profile janitor job, and appear modest.

Only, this ordinary Joe who had seen too much of the world's suffering had an extraordinary sense of justice and a quiet but relentless vengeance against those who picked on the poor and vulnerable, the people he most identified with. The unremarkable-looking Joe could slip in and out of a scene without being noticed. And when he needed to, he could draw on his extraordinary powers to inflict justice on the people most in need of it. His military training had made him an efficient and effective killer, and his deep well of inner determination made him a relentless foe.

"How did you come up with such a compelling character?" his publisher asked over dinner at a Manhattan restaurant that McElwee could never have afforded.

"Oh, you know. I just looked within. I think if we look deep enough, we all have that person inside us. That person who wants to fix the world with his secret superpowers."

"That's exactly what readers identify with." His publisher was a few years younger than him. Late thirties, he guessed. Professional, attractive, intelligent. "That sense that they have extraordinary things inside them that the world can't see behind their ordinary outward appearance. Was it painful? Did it hurt to dig that deep to find that character?"

No, thought McElwee. I just copied him from a thousand other pulp thrillers. He's a simple archetype, and a stupid one. Boil him down to his essence and you have The Incredible Hulk. Hulk see bad guy hurt nice person. Hulk get mad. Whole body puff up like erection. Bad guy get punished.

Out loud, he said, "Yeah. A little."

What hurt was that during all those years of writing intellectually honest, heartfelt stories, he couldn't make a buck. He had to scrape by teaching creative writing to undergrads—some idealistic, some self-absorbed—who would eventually go on to jobs in marketing or law or tech, vaguely holding on to the dream that they would someday write a great work of fiction that would be admired for generations.

His advice to them was always the same: Get a career. If you do well at that, you can write in your spare time.

Otherwise, you're on this hamster wheel, driving from college to college, reading endless reams of poorly written, well-intentioned prose, trying to be constructive in your feedback, trying to nurture fragile egos, trying to keep your head above water.

It's bearable when you're a drunk. Through his late twenties and early thirties, he had managed just fine. The publisher rejections hadn't yet accumulated, hadn't yet become a way of life. It got harder after he sobered up and realized how many of his high school friends had jobs, houses, spouses, kids. What bothered McElwee wasn't that they had those things, but that they could afford them, that they had choices, whereas he, at forty-three, was still living the ramen-noodle dorm room existence they'd outgrown decades ago.

McElwee fixed his eyes on the road sign ahead. One more hour to the bookstore. He'd catch up with Veronica, the owner, read for an audience of perhaps a few dozen, sign some books, then turn around and drive two hours back home through a darkening mid-December afternoon.

He'd park the car three blocks from the store. He didn't want his new audience to associate him with the old chugging Chevy, the arthritic dog belching a trail of blue smoke. He wanted them to see his new suit.

Something pained him about that, about not wanting to be associated with his own past, the past that had made him who he was. The car was the one thing in his life that had never betrayed him, and now he was embarrassed to be seen with it?

Is this what money does, he wondered. Is this the price of success? Or am I just being a sentimental sap?

# 2

He arrived early, parked the Chevy four blocks from Veronica's bookshop despite a pang of conscience at betraying his faithful servant, and justified his action by telling himself this was the closest free spot. He could have parked a block from the store, in the dollar-an-hour lot, but years of being poor had put him in the habit of counting every nickel.

When I get the Mercedes, he told himself, I'll have a valet park it.

The sky was clouding, the temperature was dropping, and he felt that rain or snow would be falling within the hour.

He seemed to get bad weather every time he came to read for Veronica. She had stuck with him through the lean years, admiring the quality of the books that creative writing professors consistently praised but that readers wouldn't buy.

Veronica had brought him in to read after the launch of each of his first three books. She must have done some legwork to hustle in the eight or ten people who showed up to listen. None of those early books earned back their paltry advances, but Veronica, bless her heart, insisted they were priceless.

Should he go in early and hang out? Catch up with his old friend?

Maybe.

Maybe if he stuck around past closing time they'd finally hook up. The possibility had hung between them since the day they'd met, fifteen-plus years ago. A little spark in the air. Or so he told himself. Realistically, if they ever did hook up, it would be out of convenience. Two lonely people getting together with someone they knew and liked and trusted well enough. It wouldn't be passionate, McElwee admitted, but if we got past the initial awkwardness, we'd both appreciate some warmth and comfort on a cold December night.

He checked his watch. Ninety minutes till the reading. Too early to drop in on Veronica. She got stressed out preparing for events like this, and she could be a nag. McElwee decided to duck into a coffee shop, get a scone and tea, and check the university app for new submissions. Of the thirty-one students in his two sections of creative writing, only six had turned in their final stories on time. The rest had taken advantage of the grace period he had offered, and today was the final day for that.

Taking a table by the window, his tea too hot to touch, he regretted his generosity in extending the deadline because it meant that when he returned to his gloomy basement apartment, he'd have a pile of papers to grade.

Well, he could do that one last time. Tabitha would curl at his feet, purr, flick her tail.

The app told him four submissions had come in last night, and twelve more this morning, including an eighty-pager at five-thirty a.m. Uh-oh, he thought. Someone pulled an all-nighter and didn't edit. And—oh no! The eighty-pager came from the nerdy philosophy major who never smiled and whose characters spoke in three-hundred-word sentences.

No matter where they were set or who the characters were, all his stories focused on some arcane philosophical conflict. The last one was about a baseball game between Cartesian dualists and Platonic idealists. Its only redeeming value was that it had cured McElwee's insomnia.

He'd left a snarky comment in the paper that he had meant to remove, an old quote from Flannery O'Connor. "Everywhere I go, people ask me if I think the universities stifle writers. In my opinion, they don't stifle enough of them."

The kid took that to the dean, and the dean put McElwee on probation.

God, how scared I was, he thought with amusement. If I had lost that job, I'd be out on the street! But now...

He licked the remains of the scone's icing from his fingertips. *Now I can tell that stupid dean to shove it. This week will be the last time I sit in that damp gloomy basement apartment plowing through hundreds of pages of dreck!*

When *Extraordinary Joe* hit the bestseller lists, friends he hadn't heard from in years flooded his Facebook page with congratulations. He didn't have an Instagram account because it was impossible to make his life look glamorous. But that was about to change. He'd fly somewhere warm, snap a photo of himself beside a palm tree, a virgin piña colada in hand with one of those little bamboo umbrellas. Maybe he could even persuade an attractive woman to pose beside him.

His old college flame, in a private Facebook message, had written, "I knew you could do it, Joe! You made it because you have heart, because you stuck it out for twenty tough years and you believed in yourself. You knew this was where you belonged and—I'm just so happy for you!"

He couldn't quite understand why her praise, which in their college days had buoyed him, now wounded him. On reading her words, he felt as he had in the Mercedes car dealer dream, like a poseur, a paper-thin fake waiting to be found out. Only, unlike the car dealers, his old college flame didn't recognize him as a phony. It would have hurt him less if she had.

She called him a day later, actually called, for the first time in ten years.

"I haven't started the new book yet, but it's on my list. I can't wait. I did take a peek inside at one of the action scenes and it totally drew me in. I mean, wow! You're like the next—"

*Oh, no,* McElwee thought. *Don't say it. Please don't say it!*

"—the next Niall Turner."

"Oh, god!" he groaned.

"No really!"

*Anyone but him,* McElwee thought. *My editor compared me to him, and my agent, and the publicist, and now you. And you all mean it as a* compliment*!*

"No, really," McElwee protested, trying to sound modest. "I'm not that—" He paused in search of the most appropriate word. Stupid? Crass? Moronic?

"I mean it," she said. "Extraordinary Joe could be the next Bronco Howitzer."

McElwee winced again. Of all Niall Turner's lowbrow creations, Bronco Howitzer was the lowest. And best selling. A macho cop who bucked the incompetent police bureaucracy to solve every problem with his fists and his gun—even cybercrime. A hyper-masculine "git 'er done" populist with all the charm and refinement of a sweaty jockstrap, he plowed through gaping plot holes like an unstoppable bulldozer. Women inexplicably fell into bed with him. Gorgeous women! Star scientists and steaming vixens whose oversized chests testified to Turner's sophomoric boob fetish.

Over time, McElwee came to understand that Turner's gratuitous sex scenes were strategically placed to stop the reader from asking questions about plot points that didn't make sense and characters who had acted out of character. How was a reader supposed to think critically when Turner was describing in excruciating detail a sex scene that read like a transcription of a bad porn video?

McElwee heard Turner had started a new series with an even stupider character, a supposedly more enlightened male detective whose contradictory traits had been designed by publisher-convened focus groups. The new series was supposedly a throwback to Raymond Chandler and the golden age of crime fiction. McElwee had avoided it on principle. Life was too short to waste on Turner novels. If he ever did look into the new series, it would be from sheer prurience, to see if the rumors were true, to see if Turner really did outdo himself by writing something even stupider than the Howitzer series.

McElwee's long silence in response to his ex-girlfriend's praise seemed to confuse her.

"Joe?"

"Huh?"

"That *is* what you wanted, right? Recognition? Respect? A bestseller?"

"Yeah," he said slowly. "I guess so."

Every time that conversation came back to him, he felt like an impostor. Now, alone in the coffee shop before his bookstore reading, something clicked in his mind. Impostor wasn't the right word. An impostor is not actually capable of what he claims to be capable of. An impostor fakes it.

Fraud was a better word. A fraud is an outright falsity. A fraud is someone who can write at McElwee's level of honesty but chooses to write like Niall— Like he-who-shall-not-be-named. A fraud swindles fools out of their hard-earned money, pretending to have a heart but really only wanting their cash.

McElwee looked at his reflection in the dark mirror of his phone screen and said aloud, "You, Joe McElwee, are a fraud."

Well, maybe so, he admitted. But look at Mae Chang. The one student in all his years of teaching who had a true gift for writing, who had stuck to her guns and published honest, thoughtful fiction, and where had it gotten her? Nowhere. She was living the same life as him, just two states over. Though her works appeared regularly in obscure literary journals, what paid her rent? Teaching freshman composition and American Lit on part-time contracts at backwater colleges that high school seniors called "safety schools." Like him, she had no health insurance.

Her recent story, "Excursion," was one of the best he had ever read. He taught it in his class as an example of how to write fiction. He praised the story for its depth and craftsmanship and hoped none of his students asked what kind of car this Mae Chang lady drove, or whether she could afford a house.

He'd heard a rumor that Niall Turner's publisher had hired her to ghostwrite a few chapters of some book recently, Turner now being too lazy to write his own work. He made outlines and farmed out the actual writing to ghostwriters with the simple instruction to stick to the Turner spirit and style. Translation: short sentences, simple characters, and no more than two consecutive chapters without a car chase, fist fight, shootout, plane crash, terrorist attack, or sex scene.

Well, if the great Mae Chang had to stoop to that to make ends meet, what shame was there in him doing the same? In fact, for once he had outdone his former student. She might have picked up a few thousand bucks on the Turner assignment. He would soon be surpassing two hundred grand for *Extraordinary Joe*, and in a few days, he'd go to New York to negotiate a new contract. He'd double down on a character and a series he didn't believe in, probably get seven figures for the US rights alone, plus more for film and streaming. And then there were the foreign rights.

After New York, he'd get that new car. And a house. No more renting. No more landlords.

Then some new clothes. And a vacation. First class, for once. To Paris, maybe. Hawaii, Cancun, Thailand. Maybe some nice restaurants for a change. I can finally tip the waitstaff and not feel like such a stingy bum.

It'll take some time to ditch the odor of poverty that I've been steeped in for so long. The rich think differently. They're not so fearful of the whims of fate, because they control so much more of their fate than the poor. They can buy their way out of the problems the rest of us have to suffer through. They can be more generous in their attitudes because their existence isn't hanging by a thread. They all have health care, and none of them are ever a paycheck away from ruin.

Having money will be a virtuous circle, he thought, the opposite of poverty's vicious circle. You're not worried all the time. Opportunity comes to you because you're open. Your spirit is generous and free, and your confidence attracts others.

That's the place you have to get to, Joe. To that place where you're at ease. Then you can stop picking on yourself. If this transition from failure to success is uncomfortable—and it is—it's only because you've been a failure for so long, you don't know how else to be. But you're going to learn. Practice, and you'll get there.

Still something nagged at him. That last Facebook message from his college ex, the private message he hadn't responded to.

*Halfway through Extraordinary Joe, and I'm sorry, but WTF?? This is garbage, Joe. Where's the heart? I don't even think I can finish it.*

She had always been brutally honest with him, and he had always respected her for that. That's what made her criticism sting.

The rain was beginning to freeze on the tree branches outside. His reading would begin in forty minutes. Veronica would be waiting, wondering where he was. He stood to leave, pulled on his coat, left the coffee shop in the wrong direction, going away from the bookstore, back toward his old Chevy.

He unlocked the passenger door, his hair wet with freezing rain, opened the glove box, removed a sheaf of papers, folded them in half lengthwise, and slid them into his coat.

He slammed the door and walked away.

Is *this* what my stupid ex-girlfriend wants to read, he muttered angrily. Because—who the hell wants to read *this*? I can't even read it myself.

The story of his marriage to Leanne was something he *had* to write, but that didn't mean it was something others needed to read. That chronicle of humiliation and dysfunction was an embarrassment he wanted to disown, a chapter of life he had tried to exorcise in writing.

So why did he have to go back to the car and get it? Why did he have to carry it inside his jacket, pressed against his heart?

He marched grimly toward the bookstore in the freezing rain, head down, angry and sullen, until he caught a glimpse of his reflection in a shop window. A decent-looking guy wearing a brand-new coat on top of the sharpest suit he'd ever owned.

Buck up, he told himself. Focus on the positive! The bad old days are over. Look forward, Joe. There's nothing but sunshine ahead!

The pep talk seemed to work. For the tenth time, he told himself his metamorphosis was beginning, his transition from loser to winner, from poverty's feelings of worthlessness and defeat to the glow of success and wealth's attractive confidence.

The usual nerves that preceded a reading faded to nothing. It didn't matter if the audience was large or small. It didn't matter if they responded to his words with enthusiasm or indifference. It didn't matter that two of his early works were soaking up rain on the dollar table outside the bookshop.

Even Veronica Wentworth's unsparing critique of his work wouldn't bother him. The bookstore owner, that avid reader with her eagle's eye for detail and her razor-sharp literary analysis—even she couldn't bring him down. Not this time. Not today.

Still, he hugged the heartfelt story to his chest like a talisman, a testament to emotional honesty and creative integrity that could shield his faltering ego against the insinuations of the Veronicas and the college exes that he had somehow sold out.

# 3

Fifty copies of *Extraordinary Joe* sat atop the table at the front of the store, upstaging even the works of Niall Turner. Granted, Turner had four novels to his one on the front table, and forty-six more on the mystery and thriller shelves in back, but McElwee for once had pride of place. His book was the centerpiece of the altar, Turner's mere acolytes bowing in reverence.

McElwee counted forty chairs, five rows of eight, facing the table in back where he would give his reading. Six seats were already occupied, while a dozen or so customers milled about, browsing the various shelves.

Forty chairs. That was optimistic for an icy, rainy day in a small town. In the past, when he was an honest nobody, he'd be happy with a turnout of eight. Back then, his audiences were thoughtful and talkative, the kinds of readers who wanted a challenge, not a formula. The kind who watched indie films that conveyed a sense of place and time and character but never seemed to go anywhere.

The readings then were cozy. The author and the audience sat in a circle, read and talked like friends, ate from the same tray of cheese and crackers, and filled their glasses from the same bottle of cheap red wine—the author in communion with his tribe.

McElwee used to eat extra during those events, took extra wine, because the food and drink were free and he was broke. Veronica understood that. She always had more food than necessary, and she lost money on all his readings. Selling two or three books didn't make up for the money she had spent on cheese and wine. But, bless her heart, she did it for the cause. The cause of *true art*, whatever that was supposed to mean.

McElwee felt a pang of nostalgia for the bad old days. The readers in that tight little circle brought his older books with them into the store with whole sections underlined and highlighted. The depth of their questions showed they had thought long and hard about what they'd read. They understood his word choice, his narrative style. They got to the beating heart beneath the prose. Some even read from their own works, and often, McElwee was moved.

Then came the letdown, the long drive back to his cold apartment, to the reality of solitude and the pile of bills he kept putting off.

Today's audience was different. A bland-looking crew who might as well have been out shopping the clearance racks at Target.

But forty seats today, not six. Forty in an icy rain! Literature was a pauper's game. *This* was commerce, the wellspring of new cars and fine wool suits!

Now Veronica approached, looking like an owl, he thought, with those great big eyes magnified by oversize glasses, and that long, thin nose. Only the hair ruined the effect, the explosion of black frizz she'd long since given up trying to control.

"Joe!" She hugged him. "How was the drive? You didn't have any trouble with the weather, did you?"

"No trouble at all." And there was that spark again. The mutual spark of attraction that never went anywhere, like a literal spark landing on wet wood.

"Listen," she whispered, casting an eye toward a woman in back, "you're not going to read a sex scene, are you? Because that one"—she glanced again to indicate the troublesome customer—"is a little uptight. And I know two people will be bringing their kids."

"Oh, no. I can't read those aloud. They make me cringe."

"Oh, good." Veronica was visibly relieved. "They make me cringe too."

"Wait, what's wrong with my sex scenes?"

"Everything, Joe." She patted his chest reassuringly. "So what are you going to read?"

"Maybe chapter two. Some good character development."

Veronica shook her head. No.

"Wait, why not?"

"Because your character has no character. Just read a chase scene, ok? Or a fight scene. And put some sound effects in it."

"What, like I'm reading a comic book?" he said playfully. "Add some *Pow!* and *Blam!* and that sort of thing?" He punched the air in sync with the sound effects.

"Yeah."

"I was joking."

"Well that's the audience you aimed for, and you hit the mark. So give them what they want."

Seeing he was stung, Veronica added, "Now's no time to develop a conscience, Joe. Think of your bank account." This time, when she patted his chest, he felt her patronizing intent.

McElwee changed his mind. Veronica *could* still bring him down. Even today.

When the reading began, only twenty-six of the forty seats were occupied. McElwee chalked it up to the weather. He thanked everyone for turning out on such a dismal day, then launched into a high-octane chase scene from chapter twelve.

When he finished, a man in the audience asked if the Dodge Charger Extraordinary Joe had hotwired to give chase was the SXT or the SRT.

McElwee was stumped. Did it matter?

"What do you mean, does it matter?" The reader, a soft, pudgy man in camouflage hunting gear who had been eating donuts throughout the reading, was upset. "A three-point-six-liter SXT and a six-point-four-liter SRT have totally different acceleration profiles. From the way the tires peeled out when Joe gunned it, I assumed it was the six-point-four."

"Ok, then," said McElwee. "The six-point-four it is."

"Well how can I be confident of that if *you* don't even know? It kinda makes me lose faith in the whole scene."

Veronica chimed in. "Sometimes these details get lost in the editing process." And then, to put the reading back on track, "Joe, how about the fight scene in chapter twenty? That's a real zinger!"

McElwee read the fight scene, in which Extraordinary Joe, fueled by righteous anger and guided by years of military training, beat up four men at once.

A fourteen-year-old boy raised his hand at the end of the passage to ask why Extraordinary Joe didn't just shoot the guys.

"Well, he can't just going around killing everyone he disagrees with," McElwee said.

"Why not?" the boy asked. "They're bad guys."

"Because," McElwee said, "then he'd be a bad guy too."

"But he kills them all later anyway."

"Yeah, but by then, they've done enough bad stuff to deserve it."

"So why not just kill 'em in the beginning?"

"Because," McElwee stammered. "Because I need time to build tension and to..." He felt himself foundering. He looked to Veronica, whose wry smile offered no support. She seemed to enjoy watching him squirm.

"It'd be a lot more efficient if Joe just killed them all up front," the kid said. "Then the bad guys wouldn't have the chance to do all that bad stuff they were going to do."

"Okay, then what would my main character do for the rest of the story?"

"Find more bad guys. Kill them too. Can you read a sex scene?"

"What? No!"

"Yeah. The one with the blonde." The kid, thumbing frantically through his book, seemed way too eager.

"I'm not reading that."

"You want *me* to read it?" asked the boy. "I'll read it!"

"No!" McElwee began to panic. Extraordinary Joe had no business with that blonde in the first place. When McElwee wrote the book, he couldn't create any chemistry between those two characters, but Extraordinary Joe had to get laid because the readers who fantasized about being an action hero also fantasized about bedding women they had no chance of ever hooking up with. Case in point, the pudgy camo guy. The sultry blonde wouldn't touch him or the fourteen-year-old with a ten-foot pole.

Oh, God, thought McElwee. What have I written?

Veronica stepped in and announced it was time for author Q&A. She lobbed some softball questions at him to take the pressure off.

*Where did the idea for the book come from?*

McElwee wiped the perspiration from his brow. The story, he said, came from one he'd read in the news about a murder and the middle-aged janitor who'd set out to avenge it.

*Were any of his characters based on real-life people?*

No. They were all made up, though some had traits of people he'd known or read about.

*Is it true there's going to be a sequel?*

Joe's publicist had instructed bookstore owners to ask this question, so the writer would have a chance to remind his audience that there was more to come.

"Why, yes! As a matter of fact..."

McElwee gave some teasers about book two, a rough draft of which languished half-written on his laptop at home. He'd been having trouble mustering the enthusiasm required for yet another shoot-'em-up, spending hours instead dreamscrolling through fantasy homes on Zillow.

After Q&A, the readers queued for him to sign copies of his breakout thriller. One man bought four copies, having each autographed for a different brother or nephew. McElwee reflected that his sales to this single individual amounted to a substantial fraction of the total sales of his first novel, a book he'd written with his soul's blood, only to find a response worse than rejection: utter indifference.

If he ever put his heart into his writing now, he kept the result to himself. Case in point, the manuscript hidden in the pocket of his coat, a thinly veiled fictional account of his failed marriage. He hadn't found a reader yet who was worth baring that part of his soul to, and even if he wanted to publish such a personal story, his editor would make him pad it out to novel length and she'd demand changes to make it more marketable.

"No," she'd say. "People *want* to see the sex. And the fights. There's something so lurid about this couple's passion and dysfunction. And everyone can identify with shame, Joe. A big swath of our readership likes to wallow in it, and an even bigger segment likes to gawk. Like, God, I know I'm bad, but at least I never sank to that!"

That, right there, was the rub, thought McElwee. He couldn't turn his heart into a commercial product. So why drag it into his work at all?

Why had it taken him so many years to learn the simple lesson of success in this business? *You don't need a heart.* The industry's publicity machine was primed to sell brand new thrillers that read just like last year's thrillers, and the mass-market audience was primed to receive them. Why work against the tide? All he had to do was see which books people were buying, and then write one of those.

Well, he did it, and he proved himself the equal of those perennial best-selling authors whose pulp novels lined the shelves of drugstores and supermarkets and Walmarts alongside the plastic frisbees and hemorrhoid cream.

McElwee lingered awhile after the audience left, catching up with his old friend Veronica, who had once hand-sold his books to customers who craved depth and meaning without knowing where to find it.

None of those early readers had come today.

"Thanks for sticking by me all these years," said McElwee without looking up from his phone.

Since his book took off, alerts came in hourly from Facebook and Twitter. His publicist managed the accounts. He never knew what she was posting until after it had gone online. And although he didn't fully understand the appeal of the vapid quotes, empty memes, and fake photos she posted, he couldn't argue with her results.

On his own, he'd struggled to muster fifty followers. For most of his early posts, he could count the shares and likes on one hand, if there were any to count at all. Now he had accumulated eighty alerts in the two hours since he'd silenced his phone. And this was a slow day for social media.

He swiped away a dozen messages from people he didn't know. Glancing up for a second, he saw Veronica standing before him with her arms crossed, her big dark owl eyes staring with disapproval.

"What?" he asked, looking back at his phone.

"When are you going to get real, Joe?"

One alert caught his eye. A direct message from an attractive young woman. *Very attractive.* Was she real, or a Russian troll? He clicked her profile.

"I spent twenty years being real," he said as he eyed a photo of a dark-haired woman in a yellow string bikini. "And no one cared."

He read the woman's name, Tatiana, and decided she was a troll.

"You know this is garbage, Joe."

Veronica had always shot straight with him, but he didn't want to hear it now.

"It's not," he replied, clicking back to the comments on his latest Twitter post. "It's just a little more commercial than my older work."

"There's a difference between being commercial and selling out," Veronica said.

He stared at a comment that consisted entirely of hearts. Thirty or forty of them at least. Why did Veronica have to be such a nag? If he wanted a conscience, he'd ask his publisher to hire one.

"Joe! I'm talking to you!"

"Sorry." He slid his phone into his pocket.

"Do you remember that game we used to play? When we'd try to dream up the most ironic punishments for the people who annoyed us?"

"Oh, yeah." He wasn't really paying attention. He was looking past her, through the window, at the bare trees glazed with ice. The rain on the pavement was beginning to freeze. If he didn't leave now, he might not make it home.

"Well you know what I think, Joe?"

He picked up his coat from the back of the chair he'd sat in during the autograph session.

"Hey," he said. "I gotta get going. This ice..."

He kissed her cheek, and his hand slid down her shoulder as he turned.

"Thanks again for setting this up," he said. "And for jumping in when the questions started going south."

The bells jingled as he opened the door to the street, the sound of gentle rain washing in on a rush of icy air. He was one step out the door when he heard her call from behind.

"I think an author who writes crappy novels should be punished by having to live inside the novel of an even crappier author."

Sour grapes, thought McElwee, tightening his coat against the rain. We can't be young and poor and idealistic forever. Someday, we have to grow up and accept the world as it is. Pay the bills and—

His foot shot forward on a patch of ice, his head pitched back violently, and the last thing he heard before the world went black was the crack of his skull against the pavement.

# Joey in the Turnerverse

4

McElwee awoke with a pounding headache and a bloody knife in his hand. On the bare floor beside him lay a pile of cash and jewels.

He sat up bleary-eyed and surveyed an empty room lit by the grey light of two large dusty windows. Holes in the plaster walls exposed ancient lath, brittle with dry rot. Outside, a lone vehicle rumbled by. Whether the growling engine belonged to car or truck, he couldn't tell.

A fragment of speech followed the noise, a woman's voice that seemed a distant memory. *I think an author who writes crappy novels...*

An author who writes crappy novels *what*, wondered McElwee. What's the rest of the sentence? He tried to blink away the pain that throbbed behind his eyes.

McElwee examined the knife and the blood that had crusted onto his hand and wrist. Then he looked at the cash. Tens of thousands of dollars, he guessed. And the jewels, they belonged to a woman. Necklaces, bracelets, rings. No loose stones. He guessed the entire haul had come from a safe.

But who keeps cash in a safe these days? And the jewels— they were ancient. Victorian, almost. Not something a young woman would wear.

*...should be punished by having to live inside the novel of an even crappier author.*

He dropped the knife, rubbed his aching head. Who had said that? Who was a crappy author? Who needed to be punished?

He looked again around the room. No furniture. Just an open door to an adjoining room. And then an apparition. A striped cat with bright green eyes.

Tabitha!

She arched her back and rubbed her side against the doorframe, tail straight up, and announced her desire to eat with a rolling meow that curled into a question, Rrrrr-now?

How did *she* get here?

He stood slowly, seeing stars, wobbled on his feet for a moment, then stepped unsteadily toward the door.

What was in the other room, he wondered. And then, looking down, where did I get these shoes?

They were too small. He wore a twelve. These couldn't have been bigger than nines. But they didn't pinch, even though they ended in a narrow point.

"What *is* this?" he asked aloud, as he lifted his leg and wrenched the shoe from his foot. "Some Italian designer crap?"

He read the label inside. Sbadiglio.

"Christ!" He hurled the shoe across the room, startling the cat, who fled through the open door.

He pulled off the other shoe, tossed it, and rubbed his toes.

They felt wrong. Too small, just like his hands and fingers.

He had given up drinking eight years earlier because of mornings like this, though this one seemed worse than even the worst of the old days. Waking up in a strange place? Sure. That had happened plenty of times, though usually there was a woman beside him. When he awoke before her, he'd play a little game with himself, trying to remember how they'd met and what her name was.

If she woke up first, she was usually showered by the time his eyes opened. His clothes would sit neatly folded beside the bed, left there not by him the night before, but by her just now. An invitation to leave. He'd play his game alone on the way home. What was her name? Where were we last night?

This morning reaffirmed for him just how glad he was to be done with that life. Perhaps his distorted perception was his brain's way of getting back at him, as if to say, "Oh, you're going to poison me again? Well then, *this* is what I'm going to do to your world."

*This* being the disconcerting sensation that his body was all wrong, hands and feet and toes too small. He even felt shorter than normal. How was that possible?

And now something else. He used to have a dusting of dark brown hair on the backs of his hands, and on the first joints of his fingers. Now the hair was gone.

Had he shaved? Why would he do that?

He turned toward the dingy window and examined his hands in the dull morning light. Either his vision was blurry or his skin had smoothed out. And he definitely had not shaved the backs of his hands. Where the sprouts of dark hair used to be, he saw fine golden down, too light and thin to be visible except at close range.

"Rrrrr-now?" purled the cat.

"Ok, I'm coming."

He turned from the window, crossed the bare floor, passed through the door into the kitchen and made an inventory. Round Formica table with two orange-padded chrome-lined chairs and a red and orange swirl pattern on top. Late 1960s or early '70s, he thought. Bare, off-white, laminated counter crisscrossed with meandering golden lines. Seventies? Maybe earlier.

The front of the undersized fridge was rounded like a midcentury Chevy. Nineteen fifties, he thought. The white electric stove could be a decade older or younger than the fridge.

On the stove's back burner, a percolator. On the counter, an empty coffee cup, a tumbler with half an inch of light brown liquid. Probably whiskey and melted ice left over from the night before.

Beside the glass, a bottle of I.W. Harper's. McElwee, once a connoisseur of all things alcoholic, noted it should have said "I.W. Harper," without the apostrophe S. Cheap knockoff whiskey. No wonder his head hurt so bad.

"Rrrrr-now?" asked the cat, rubbing her side against the fridge.

An electric can opener, vintage 1960, stood beside the sink. And next to it, ten small cans stacked in a neat pyramid. The labels, black block letters on a field of empty white, said "Cat Food."

McElwee picked up a can and turned it around as the purring cat slithered between his ankles. The back of the label was empty. No ingredients or sell-by date, no manufacturer name or bar code.

A strange, uncanny feeling washed over him. The generic labels, the mismatched furnishings—these had come from the props department of some film studio or playhouse. The other room, with its peeling plaster and grimy windows, its rumbling cliché of the passing car, its wide, bare floor—that was a stage.

The bloody knife, the pile of cash and jewels—who piles those things on the floor? This was a set piece, the work of a hack director who had just enough rudimentary understanding of storytelling to set a scene.

He dashed back into the main room, expecting to see the seats of an auditorium, an audience watching him there on stage. That would explain this joke and put his mind at ease.

But relief didn't come. The room's four solid walls trapped him inside what was beginning to feel like a nightmare.

The pounding in his temples eased for a moment and he became lightheaded. His stomach dropped, and the room began to spin. Was there a bathroom here? Could he find it before he puked?

He staggered back to the kitchen, his guts heaving. There, to the right, a second door. He stumbled through, half-blind, bumping the doorframe on his way in. If it hadn't been there to check him, he would have crashed sideways against the sink.

The bowl of the toilet rushed up to swallow him. His insides emptied out and he saw stars.

A moment later, as he came back to his senses, he felt the cool porcelain on his arms. He wondered if during his drinking days he had developed an instinct to find the magic bowl, even while blind and senseless. He wondered if a non-drinker, someone without his vast, regrettable experience, would have thrown up all over the floor.

The inside of the bowl was an ugly sight. McElwee studied it to see if any intact bits of food could give him a clue about what he'd eaten last night. That might jog his memory and help him figure out where he'd been. But the stench was as nauseating as the sight. He turned his head away and flushed, one arm still resting on the toilet rim.

Looking around the room as the filth swirled down, he saw a generic white porcelain pedestal sink, circa 1940. White hexagon floor tiles, each an inch and a half wide. Shiny white square tiles on the walls, ending in a single row of shiny black tiles four feet above the floor. Bare bulb on ceiling. Metal tub with exposed pipe rising from the tap to a broad showerhead. Dingy white cloth curtain pulled open on a curved chrome bar. All generic, low-budget clichés.

Above the sink, a medicine cabinet. The door was open, exposing empty glass shelves.

McElwee unspooled two feet of toilet paper and wiped his face. He stood slowly, dropping the wad of paper into the bowl, which he flushed again, hoping to wash away the final remains of whatever the hell he did last night.

The sink, he thought, was too high. The toilet too, for that matter. Either the props department had got the dimensions wrong or he really was shrinking.

The mirror above the sink, he told himself, the mirror on the other side of that wide-open medicine cabinet door, would be cracked. Whoever furnished this place was too unimaginative or too lazy to think beyond the tired tropes of old Hollywood.

He shut the cabinet door and took a moment to study the unfamiliar face staring back at him from both sides of the mirror's long diagonal crack.

"My God," he said softly, stroking the dark stubble of his chiseled cheek. "I'm fucking gorgeous!"

# 5

The cars on the street outside, like the suit he'd found in the closet after showering, were from the 1940s. But, like the fine wool slacks that brushed against his thighs, they hadn't aged. A few were shiny enough to have come directly from the showroom.

The streetlamps too were of an ancient style, possibly converted from gas lamps, though they hadn't aged either. The tall palms that lined the sidewalks told him he was in Southern California. Los Angeles, he guessed.

He looked back at the rundown building he'd just exited. The name etched in sandstone above the door: The Loaded Arms.

Who names a building that?

And what kind of neighborhood was this, where the buildings were rundown but the cars were new?

The bar across the street, a dive, was closed. The strip club beside it was open. A sleepy bouncer in a shoddy grey suit leaned against the doorframe, his dark fedora tilted to the side.

McElwee removed the fedora from his own head and examined it. The felt was crisp and new, the black silk band still had a slick sheen. The hat matched the dark blue of his suit, which had been custom tailored to hug his waist and shoulders.

The suit and hat and Italian leather shoes made him feel foolish, like a pint-size playboy lost on the wrong side of town, a target inviting attack. The sooner he left here, the better.

He pulled his hat down to his eyebrows, put his hands in his pockets, turned left, and walked briskly, keeping his head down to avoid eye contact with anyone who might take offense at being looked at. He didn't stop to think about which direction to go. Not knowing where he was, one direction was as good as another. The important thing was to get away from the bloody knife, the money, and the jewels that had obviously been stolen.

He did take note of his direction. It was morning, and the sun was behind him. He was heading west. Good to know, in case he needed to return.

But why would he return? Somewhere in the dull mists of his mind was a reason to go back, or else he wouldn't have thought of it.

Right, the cat! Tabitha was still in the apartment. He would return for her once he'd gotten a good meal in his stomach and was able to think straight.

He stopped at the corner and read the street sign. Sixth and Murder. The Loaded Arms was on Murder Row. He should make a note of that. Details were hard to hold on to in the fog of his hangover, in the fog of... whatever had made his head ache so badly.

He reached instinctively for his phone in the inside pocket of his jacket. He pulled instead a sheaf of twenty pages, unfolded them and took a look.

Oh, no! That! That bit of his past he had tried unsuccessfully to purge in a spew of anguished words. That woeful tale of his failed marriage, a chapter of his life he wanted to edit out. Why was he carrying this in his jacket? Was there a garbage can on this godforsaken street?

He scanned the sidewalks. They *were* the garbage can, the curbs and gutters littered with cigarette butts, empty match boxes, chewing gum wrappers, tickets of some kind. He couldn't throw his heart out here. As little as he thought of himself, his soul was not yet in the gutter.

He refolded the papers and put them back in his jacket pocket, then searched the other pocket for his phone.

What was this? A wallet. Black snakeskin.

He kept walking as he opened it. None of his credit cards were inside. Just two laminated cards, and two bills: a twenty and a ten.

He stopped, looked around to make sure no pickpockets or thugs were nearby, then pulled a wad of twenties and fifties from his pocket and stuffed them into the wallet. The cash had come from the pile of stolen loot inside the bare apartment. He'd taken some for spending money so he could get a bite to eat in this strange place.

He walked again, pulling one of the cards from the wallet. A driver's license. That was his face in the photo. Not his proper face, but the handsome one he had seen in the mirror half an hour earlier.

The name on the license said Joey Sternjaw. That had to be a joke.

Address, 123 Terra. No street or avenue or lane. Just Terra. Another joke.

And the license listed his height as five foot six. His heart skipped a beat. Ever since that first look in the mirror, he'd been assuring himself he was at least five nine.

Even five nine was hard to swallow. He hadn't been that short since middle school. He had reached his full height of six feet in tenth grade, and now he'd been demoted.

Five foot six?

He'd be looking up at the chins of the taller women he preferred. How could they take him seriously?

And in a bad neighborhood like this? He glanced at the haggard man in the rumpled suit sleeping on the bus stop bench. In a neighborhood like this, where the weak were prey, how could he defend himself?

He shoved the card back into the wallet, and the wallet into the jacket.

Up ahead, an old man, bald and stooped, was unlocking the door of a shop. As McElwee approached, the man held the door open for him and said, "Notebooks, aisle three. Pencils right next to 'em."

"Thanks," said McElwee.

How did he know? How did the old man know I was thinking about buying a notebook?

He found one in aisle three, the flip-top kind that cops and detectives and reporters used to carry in the breast pockets of their jackets in old Hollywood films. All the pencils in the bins were of yellow wood, none of the plastic mechanical type he preferred.

He picked a short one, the size of a golf pencil. It had no eraser, but it would fit in his pocket better than the long ones.

When the cashier rang up the sale—six cents—McElwee put down a twenty.

The old man looked up at him. "Got anything smaller?"

"A ten," McElwee said, rummaging through his wallet.

"Ah, what's the point?"

The cashier took the twenty and counted out nineteen dollars and ninety-four cents in change.

Exiting the store, McElwee wrote his first notes:

- The Loaded Arms
- Sixth and Murder
- Joey Sternjaw
- Five foot six, 140 pounds :(
- Tabitha

He'd get the cat after he ate. Yes, after he ate at the diner down the street, he'd get the cat and look for 123 Terra. Maybe it was a real place. Maybe whoever set him up with the knife and the cash and the jewels and the suit had also made a home for him.

Maybe 123 Terra would be less of a nightmare than the dump he woke up in. Or maybe it would be worse.

# 6

The red neon sign above the diner said Sicora's. Beneath that, in blue neon, "Burgers, Shakes, Breakfast 24 Hours."

As McElwee approached the entrance, a black Cadillac glided to a stop at the curb, followed by a yellow Packard. The Caddy, a 1940s model, glistened like new. The sputtering yellow Packard stopping behind it was older. Its skinny tires suggested 1920s.

The rear door of the Caddy and all four doors of the Packard opened in unison. From the Cadillac emerged a tall, thin man wearing a suit as sharp as McElwee's. His hair was parted on the side and slicked down with gel. His face, overconfident to the point of smugness, was lit with a wolfish grin.

If he was a gangster or a boss, the four burly men in t-shirts piling out of the Packard were his thugs. The biggest and dumbest looking of them all, a balding dark-haired man with a protruding Neanderthal brow and muscles like overstuffed sausage, pointed a stumplike finger at McElwee and asked the boss if "dat" was him.

"That's him," said the boss. "Go introduce yourself." And then to McElwee, the boss added, "Polski's new."

The boss and the other three brutes from the Packard watched as Polski approached his target with a bully's swaggering confidence.

McElwee turned and looked around him, not knowing what to do. If ever there was a time when my real height would come in handy, he thought...

He noticed that the customers in the diner were watching, though he could see from their faces no one would come to help him. Their expressions showed more amusement than concern. They were going to be treated to a show. In this down-at-the-heels neighborhood, he thought, watching someone else take a beating, instead of having to take one yourself, was a form of entertainment.

"Hey there, little fella!"

McElwee turned to see the giant Polski, who must have been six foot six, bending down and grinning. "Is your daddy home?"

Polski's big doughy face was red and pockmarked. His breath, hot and close, smelled like coffee and tuna fish.

The big man straightened up, still grinning, and lifted the hat off McElwee's head, crumpling it and yanking out a few hairs along the way.

He threw the hat on the pavement and stomped on it, his eyes fixed on McElwee, looking for the reaction of terror and helplessness he seemed to crave.

To his surprise, McElwee did not lose his cool. He had never been particularly brave, at least not physically. He liked to think he had some moral courage—and according to his friends and exes, he did—but when it came to physical confrontations, he found himself weak in the stomach. Until today, his saving graces had been his physical size and his ability to hide his fear.

Polski seemed more amused than frustrated by the little man's lack of distress. With a sneer, he said, "Oh, did the little king lose his crown?"

He bent down, picked up the hat, and dusted it off with the back of his hand in an exaggerated act of showmanship, as if playing to the audience peering through the diner windows.

"Here you go, sweetie," he said in the tone of a mother addressing her little girl.

He raised the hat above McElwee's head and brought it down with a piledriver of a fist, sending a shockwave through the little man's skull and straight down his spine.

The last time McElwee had been hit like this was in fourth grade. The boy doing the hitting was in eighth, and McElwee had wet himself in front of his classmates. Granted, they had sympathy. They were on his side. But the humiliation burned for years.

This time, he surprised himself by throwing a lightning fast and shockingly powerful right hook to Polski's solar plexus. The big man dropped to the pavement, gasping in a fetal position while the Cadillac boss and the three Packard thugs roared with laughter.

McElwee felt pity for the man on the ground, whose face was crumpled in agony, right leg twitching uncontrollably, as if trying to kick out the pain.

The Cadillac boss grinned at McElwee and said, "Breaking in the new guy."

One of the other thugs helped Polski up off the ground. As the man walked his injured comrade back to the Packard, McElwee heard him say, "First rule of battle with Joey Sternjaw: Bring a gun."

The men got back in their cars and drove off as inexplicably as they had appeared.

McElwee would add this encounter to his notes over breakfast. He wondered how long it would take for the basic ground rules of this universe to make sense. Already, he feared he'd need a bigger notebook.

7

The counter inside the diner stood to the left, tables to the right. Black and white floor, white counter, white tables. The stools and chairs alternated. Black, white, black, white. All had chrome tubing, and all were worn.

Art Deco, McElwee thought. This would have been a high-end joint in the 1930s. If the decade matches the cars outside, we're in the '40s, and this neighborhood has gone downhill since the diner was built.

A few customers smiled at him. Men in baggy grey rumpled suits, workmen in blue jumpsuits, women not yet caffeinated enough to wash the sleep from their eyes.

"Nice one," said the woman behind the counter.

"Thanks." McElwee strained to read the black nametag on her white uniform. Jean.

"You know he'll come back for you," she said.

McElwee took a seat at the counter, hoping that wasn't true and fearing it was. He wasn't sure how to respond to the woman's remark. Part of him felt that Jean, who apparently knew him, expected him to come back with a tough guy wisecrack. Part of him wanted to make one, to say something like, "Not if he knows what's good for him." He would be able to gauge from Jean's response whether his attitude was on target; whether, in this world, people knew better than to mess with Joey Sternjaw.

In the end, he said nothing, out of fear of exposing the fact that he didn't know who he was. Jean turned to get a pot of coffee, turned back to fill his cup, smiling shyly as she poured. Her nervous attraction told him that his enigmatic silence had been the right response. He was properly in character for whomever he was supposed to be.

44

He picked up the menu and scanned the breakfast list, surprised to find himself craving heavy, greasy food. He couldn't think of anything more satisfying than a plate of scrambled eggs, hash browns, sausage, bacon, and ham, even though he didn't eat meat anymore.

Back in his drinking days, he had mysteriously ballooned up to 256 pounds. Mysterious to him. And mysterious only while he was still drinking.

When he sobered up, he started counting the calories of his nightly binges. Twelve or fifteen drinks added up to three full meals in liquid form. And the daily hangovers changed his appetite. He started craving cheeseburgers, bacon cheeseburgers, huge plates of sausage and eggs. Heavy, fattening foods to tamp down the throbbing nerves.

After he stopped drinking, he started eating oatmeal for breakfast, salads and stir-fries for lunch, veggies and pasta or rice for dinner. Part of the dietary change, he admitted, was economic. He was always broke, and pasta, rice, and oatmeal were cheap. But the change did him good. He stopped craving heavy foods and suspected he could no longer stomach them.

He dropped fifty-six pounds in his first year sober, down to an even two hundred, and his weight had stayed there for eight straight years now. Not bad for his real-life height of six feet. He had more energy at a sober forty than he'd had at a drunken thirty.

Yet now, here he was, hungover again—or feeling like it, anyway—craving grease, and from the looks of himself in the cracked bathroom mirror an hour ago, he was probably age thirty again.

Actually, he thought, how old *am* I?

Jean slid a plate of scrambled eggs, hash browns, bacon, sausage, and ham in front of him just as he was putting down the menu.

"I don't know why you bother reading that," she said. "You order the same thing every time you come in."

As he pulled his wallet from his jacket, McElwee made a mental note to make a written note about having been in

Sicora's Diner before. He slid the driver's license from the wallet and read the date of birth. 1917.

If he was at home in the right universe, he'd be a hundred and six. In this place, where the year seemed to be sometime in the 1940s, he probably was about thirty.

He thought of a quick experiment. Turn around, scan the crowd. If there's anyone in military uniform, we're in the war years, 1942 to 1945. He turned and looked at the customers, the same men in suits and jumpsuits he'd seen before. No uniforms though. Either the US had not entered the war yet, or the country was past it. That meant—assuming the birth date on his license was correct—he was either under twenty-five or over twenty-nine.

What about the women? If he knew anything about hairstyles, he might have been able to guess the year from those. Unfortunately, he knew just enough to tell the difference between 1990s, '80s, and '70s. He could identify some of the '60s dos that required a full can of spray to hold in place, but anything before that he simply lumped into the category of "black-and-white movie era." He used to marvel at the old family photos in which young women framed pretty faces with unflattering hairdos that made them look a decade older than they were.

The woman at the table nearest him wore a white blouse and blue skirt. Her brown hair was frizzed and splayed, like a hairdo that had come apart. He took the man beside her to be her husband because the two ate in silence and didn't look at each other.

Behind that couple, a woman sat with three men. All wore the dark blue jumpsuits of factory workers. That told him the year was at least 1946. Women had gone into the factories during the war, not before. And able-bodied young men would have been in the military, not on the factory floor, if the war was still on.

Could he glean information from anyone else?

Yes. The sultry redhead in the corner booth smoking a cigarette. Fair-skinned, boobs too big for her green satin dress.

Her voluptuous elegance was grossly out of place in this greasy skid-row dive. She didn't even have food on her table. She stared at him with an alluring insolence he told himself he wasn't going to respond to.

When he turned back to his food, Jean said, "Looks like you have a fan."

"You noticed her too?"

"She's been staring a hole right through you, Joey."

Jean dropped a copy of the morning paper next to his plate and said, "Are you already working this case? 'Cause if you're not, you know it's going to drop into your lap. Unless you have to recuse yourself because of Dorothy. Do PIs have to recuse themselves? Like judges? Is that a thing?"

McElwee ignored the blaring front page headline and checked the date under the masthead. June 1, 1948. That would make him thirty-one years old.

The *Los Angeles Examiner*, as far as he knew, was not a real paper. But then, neither was the five-foot-six Joey Sternjaw a real person.

The headline said, "Lady Astor Robbed, Murdered." The photo below showed an open, empty safe among the shelves of a mansion's richly appointed library. McElwee extrapolated from the sizes of the surrounding books that the safe was large enough to hold the pile of cash and jewels he'd left back in the bare apartment.

He dug into his eggs as he read the article. Lady Agatha Astor of Beverly Hills had been stabbed to death in her library. The safe had been opened using the combination; it had not been forced. Police suspected the victim may have opened it herself. She may have known or trusted her attacker. Police said the stolen loot included a substantial amount of cash and jewelry, though they declined to name an amount or to describe the jewels.

As McElwee looked up to see a burly middle-aged detective entering the diner, he could feel the eyes of the woman in green burning into the back of his head.

He knew the man approaching him was a detective because, like the crime boss and the goons outside, like the sultry femme fatale behind him, like all the features of the rundown apartment in The Loaded Arms, this man was a stereotype. The rumpled suit, the outdated wool hat—outdated even for 1948—the gut hanging over his belt, the no-nonsense, world-weary face that suggested duty came first, sleep second...

This lazily drawn trope of the classic crime novel was the sidekick sent off by the main character—another investigator—to track down some minor hoodlum from whom he'd extract a clue in a dark alley or a dive bar or a shooting gallery. McElwee had a name for him. The dedicated and reliable Frump. However haggard and worn-out he looked, he always managed to get his little bit of the job done, and the reader only ever saw him coming or going. Whatever he did in the alley or the dive bar or the shooting gallery to make people talk was beyond the reader's concern, and the writer's.

As the Frump made a beeline for him, McElwee wondered who Dorothy was. He couldn't ask Jean, because the way she had mentioned her, Dorothy was obviously someone familiar. And if there was any question of him recusing himself from the Astor investigation on Dorothy's account, that meant he and Dorothy and Lady Agatha Astor were all somehow connected.

Remembering the bloody knife, the pile of cash and jewels, McElwee's heart began to race. Was the disheveled detective coming to interrogate him? To arrest him?

To reassure himself, McElwee took his wallet from his jacket and pulled out the second card, the one he hadn't yet looked at. He read it as Detective Frump planted himself on the adjoining stool.

*Joey Sternjaw, Private Investigator.* The card included a license number and the official seal of the city of Los Angeles.

Frump put his hand on McElwee's shoulder, leaned in close, and said, "What's *she* doing here?"

At "she," he jerked his thumb back toward the sultry woman in green.

McElwee meant to say he didn't know—because, honestly, he didn't—but what came out was, "It's a free country."

"Sure it is," said Frump, giving him a too-hard pat on the back. "I assume, since you're down here, Dorothy already hired you."

"Um..." McElwee didn't know how to respond to that. If he said yes and was wrong, or if he said no and was wrong, he'd have to explain that later to the cops. Or at least to Detective Frump, who was now asking Jean for a cup of coffee.

"The jewels were insured for two million," Frump said in a low voice. "Which probably means they were worth one. The rich always inflate the values on their policies. The cash—you know how much that was?"

"How much?" McElwee asked as he lifted his coffee cup to his lips.

"Seventy-eight thousand."

"Shit!"

"Pardon?" Frump looked surprised.

"I said, shit. That's a lot of money."

Frump leaned in and said in an even lower voice, "Watch your mouth, Joey."

"Huh?"

"That's a bad guy word."

"Bad guy?"

"If you want to express surprise, you can just whistle. You know, just let out a long whistle like, phew! That's a lot of dough." Frump patted his shoulder like an uncle giving advice to a clueless teen.

"Ok. You, uh, have any leads?"

"Nothing yet. But I wanted to pass along a clue. Take a look at this." Frump pulled an eight-by-ten photo from a manila envelope.

"Where did you get that?" McElwee asked.

"Police photographer took it at the crime scene."

"No, the envelope. You didn't have it when you walked in."

"Didn't I?" Frump seemed surprised.

"No. I saw both your hands. They were empty."

Frump shrugged. "Just a glitch, I guess. You're not supposed to dwell on it."

Not *supposed* to dwell on it? Are there rules here about what I'm supposed to perceive and what I'm supposed to ignore?

McElwee felt a deep unease creep through his veins. Waking up with a bloody knife in hand, not knowing where he was, the strange face in the mirror, his implication in this murder-robbery—all of it had been unnerving, but not in the way this was, because this, the envelope, was *real*. An actual physical object had appeared from nowhere, and he was supposed to ignore it.

Something in his subconscious told him the "glitch" of the manila envelope was, in fact, the reason he was here. He felt it as a visceral truth.

Wait a minute, he thought. I made that mistake a few times in *Extraordinary Joe*, forgetting to place a key element in a scene, then having it appear from nowhere. My editor caught most of the errors, but one slipped into publication, and my readers complained about it.

He turned instinctively, as if for help, to the woman in green. She smiled, gave him a little wave of the fingers, a gesture that struck him as girlish and out of character for a woman who exuded such erotic power.

She mouthed something at him. He read her lips so clearly, he could almost hear the words. "Waking up now, are we?"

Once again, he heard in his mind those strange words whose origin he couldn't place. *An author who writes crappy novels should be punished by having to live inside the novel of an even crappier author.*

"Don't look at her, Joey." That was Frump. "You know better than to get mixed up with her kind. Look at this."

Frump showed him a photo of a bloody footprint on the marble floor of Lady Astor's library.

"That's from a boot. Size twelve," Frump said. "We've never seen that tread before."

Of course you haven't, McElwee thought. That pattern didn't exist until the twenty-first century. That print came from the ribbed sole of one of the derby dress shoes he'd bought to go with his two new suits.

And with that memory came a breakthrough, the first detail he could recall from the haze of confusion that preceded his arrival in this strange world. His leather derby, the left one, size twelve, was shooting away from him on a patch of icy pavement. And then...

And then, what? There was no next thing.

He still didn't know how he had gotten here, but boy did his head ache!

8

Twenty minutes later, he returned to find the apartment at The Loaded Arms empty. The cash, the jewels, the cat, and the whiskey were all gone. All that remained was the cat food. That disturbed McElwee. Whoever had taken Tabitha didn't seem too concerned about feeding her. Her normal temperament ranged from aloof to demure to playful, but she became savagely ill-tempered when denied food. He hoped her captors would keep her around long enough to suffer her wrath.

Let's calm down here, he told himself. Let's take a breath and try to work out what's going on. I wake up in a strange world full of tropes. They're crime fiction tropes, familiar stuff, but not well thought out. The work of a crappy author.

Okay, let's run with that. Let's say I'm in someone else's book, because no other explanation makes sense. Whose book is this? And what are the rules? Because until I figure those out, I'm just going to be confused, and I might even get myself killed.

Let's start, he told himself, like we used to do in high school English class. Make an inventory of the scene, see what we can glean from that. What can we tell about this author from the world he's created?

At the kitchen table, he sat and wrote in his notebook.

The first thing he noted was the table itself. It was definitely not from the 1940s. He had had one like it in his kitchen growing up. His parents had bought it when they married, in the 1970s, during that inscrutable era when people thought red and orange went together and looked just fine in the kitchen.

He crouched down and found on the underside of the table a printed label that said *Made in Tiewon*. Taiwan wasn't a country until the late '40s, and America wasn't importing substantial goods from there until the '60s or '70s. Also, it was spelled Taiwan, not Tiewon.

The author of this universe was careless, McElwee decided, if not downright sloppy. Nothing annoyed him more than reading a book where the details didn't add up. He hoped not to find any more such lapses, and wondered for a moment if he should stop looking too closely at things.

Then he wondered if that was even possible. His readers had always praised his eye for detail. It wasn't something he could turn off, any more than he could turn off his ability to see color or hear a tune.

Ok, he told himself. Enough nitpicking. Let's get to the bigger things.

There was something familiar about the woman in green, though he was certain he had never met her before. She knew something, and she wanted him to know she knew something, but what she knew was anyone's guess.

Judging by what he had learned so far—that he was a detective, that this was 1940s Los Angeles, that she was gorgeous and teasing and disliked by Frump—he was sure to run into her again. A tingle of anticipation ran through him as he thought about what happened between well-intentioned detectives and sultry seductresses in 1940s pulp fiction.

Next, he noted the name of the thug who had attacked him. Polski. He thought about that for a moment. Polski looked and sounded Polish. The name wasn't very imaginative.

The author who neglected to furnish the apartment, who labeled his cat food cans "Cat Food," was as lazy with names as he was with descriptions.

Then again, thought McElwee, he could be an intelligent author writing for a stupid audience. Polski conveyed the ethnicity of the character as clearly as "Cat Food" conveyed the contents of the can.

When he'd made the move from literary failure to successful thriller writer, McElwee learned that genre readers zipping through the pages of cookie-cutter novels had to be reminded of important details every now and then, or they'd lose the thread of the plot, and plot was king.

His public reading reaffirmed this truth again and again. On his book tour, he had encountered hordes of obtuse readers who grasped only the broadest outlines of plot and character. They had to be reminded of details repeatedly, because their minds were dozing even when their eyes were open.

So maybe the author of this dim-witted world wasn't lazy or stupid after all. Maybe he had simply figured out how much pablum he could load onto the mass-market spoon without choking his audience. Whether the author of this world was hopelessly incompetent or shrewdly cunning required further observation. For now, McElwee would withhold judgment.

Now another thought came to him. When he had stood to leave the diner, Frump reached into his pocket for change to pay for the coffee. Pushing aside his jacket, he revealed the badge on his belt. It said "Det. Frump."

"That's your real name?" McElwee asked.

"What? Like you don't already know? Come on, Joey!"

Frump was just a tag McElwee had put on the detective, a label for someone whose name he didn't know. And yet that had become his actual name.

McElwee shook his head, wrote "Authorial laziness," and underlined it twice. Then he thought again and added, "Good shorthand. Gives the reader a physical picture to hold on to, and also reflects his tired, disheveled character."

He then noted the manila envelope that Frump seemed to have produced from thin air, as well as Frump's admonition against looking too far into that inconsistency. That was straight-up bad writing, like a magician telling his audience to watch his right hand, not his left.

It got worse.

McElwee noted that whoever had cleared out the apartment had left a big stinking present in the toilet. They had cleaned the blood from the floor in the main room. And they appeared to have fixed the mirror. It was no longer cracked.

Why would anyone do that? It made no sense.

The only explanation was that the author had forgotten about the details of the blood and the mirror, and when he redrew the apartment for McElwee's re-entry, he forgot to add those bits.

Had this kind of error occurred in McElwee's own writing? It had indeed. His recent bestseller had had a dozen chapters cut, moved, shortened, lengthened, or entirely rewritten. Inconsistencies had crept in during the upheaval. The publisher stuck to a rigid production schedule, so the book went to press before some of the conflicting minor details could be corrected. Some obnoxious reader had written a blog post about all of the inconsistencies. McElwee wasn't sure which upset him more: the embarrassing gaffes or the fact that most of his readers ignored them.

He sighed and was about to shut the notebook when something new occurred to him. He should have seen it before. His handwriting was his own. Unlike his face, his height, his name, the decade, and everything else in this universe, his handwriting had not changed.

He put his pencil to the pad, closed his eyes, and imagined he was signing a check. Joseph E. McElwee.

That felt natural. But when he opened his eyes, the signature, in his own familiar hand, said Joey Sternjaw.

He tried it again and got the same result.

Why was the name Joey Sternjaw beginning to sound familiar?

Another memory flashed before his mind, visually vague but emotionally clear: a woman whom he liked and disliked. She sat across a table from him (a dinner table?) and said the name Joey Sternjaw. He told her she was crazy, though inwardly her words had stung.

What did the woman look like? Thin face, long nose, dark frizzy hair, and glasses that magnified her already too-large eyes. She criticized him and stared too much, a big staring owl, picking at his flaws, and he wanted her to shut up and sleep with him.

She was not attractive, but she was obtainable, and that made him want her, even though she annoyed him.

Obtainable and unattractive, staring too much and telling him things he didn't like to hear, she was maddeningly intelligent and insightful, her comments always on the mark.

He tried to recall more of their conversation, but she vanished from his mind's eye—deliberately, he thought, out of spite. And she seemed to have taken with her the whole world in which she appeared, the world McElwee considered his true and proper universe. The one where events made sense, where the rules weren't as arbitrary as they were here.

He couldn't remember anything else about their encounter, however hard he tried. Where were they? What was on the table? What had they been talking about, besides Joey Sternjaw?

McElwee stood from the table and closed the notebook. He looked for a phone, but the apartment didn't have one.

On the street out front, he turned left again, toward the diner. The number of businesses in that direction seemed to increase the farther he went. Stores, restaurants, bars. Where there were businesses, there would be taxis. It took him six blocks and twenty-one minutes to find one. A yellow Ford, late 1930s, with a rounded body and big teardrop fenders.

The cabbie rolled to a stop, leaned toward the open passenger window, and said, "Where to, Mac?"

"Mac?"

"Sorry," said the cabbie. "Sir."

McElwee was at first heartened by the familiar address. His old college friends called him Mac. Then came the disappointment. Mac was a generic form of address in the films of the '30s and '40s. Another cliché. A trope, or an act of imaginative laziness, like the big Polish brute being called Polski.

"So where will it be?" asked the cabbie.

"123 Terra," McElwee said as he slid into the back seat.

"Gotcha!" The driver flipped the meter and hit the gas.

# 9

Winding north through the city, McElwee took in the sights of late 1940s Los Angeles. In his mind, the cars of the '40s were all black, because that's how they appeared in the old films. But on the streets, though black predominated, he saw of number of green, yellow, and red cars, along with an occasional blue.

He considered for a moment that this might not be an accurate representation. The anachronism of the table and chairs in the apartment's kitchen still bothered him. Those were definitely from the 1970s. And then there was the whiskey bottle. I.W. Harper's, with its extraneous apostrophe S. If the author of this universe had been wrong about those details, he could be wrong about the cars as well.

The streets were broad and sunny, and the houses in whatever neighborhood he was currently passing through were small. In the twenty-first century, these would be called starter homes. One story, two bedrooms, with a small porch and yard.

The people on the sidewalks—women with strollers, men walking God knows where—were better dressed than the people of his day and age, though they didn't always look better for it. Why?

The women wore skirts and blouses. Men wore slacks, button-down shirts, and some even had vests. But the clothes didn't always fit well. Nor were they well made, he noted as the taxi stopped at an intersection to let a group of pedestrians cross.

He remembered his grandfather telling him that for years, he owned only two sets of clothes: one for work and one for church. Clothing loses its crispness when worn too often. It gets threadbare, with a slack, almost slovenly look.

Every man on the street wore a hat, and many of the women too. When did that stop, he wondered.

When Martin Luther King led his March on Washington, all the men wore hats. Then he was killed. 1968. After that, McElwee was hard-pressed to find a hat on anyone. In the photos of crowds from the '70s and '80s, no one wore hats, unless you count baseball caps and cowboy hats. The fedoras were all gone. And so were the manners, he thought. And, to some extent, civility in general.

Rolling into North Hollywood, the houses got a little bigger. Nothing like the suburban McMansions of the early twenty-first century, but definitely roomier and better built than the cracker boxes he'd been looking at a few minutes earlier. These were craftsman and Cape Cod houses of three or even four bedrooms. More than just boxes to put people in, they were homes with an actual aesthetic vision, in which young couples began lives of modest fulfillment rather than lives of scraping by.

The driver pulled up in front of what looked like an English country cottage. The brown stone facade was out of step with the rest of the houses on the block, which were all made of wood.

"123 Terra," he said. Without turning around, he held his hand palm-up over his shoulder to collect the fare. The meter said $2.75. McElwee handed him a five and told him to keep the change.

He stood on the sidewalk for a moment assessing the house, the cab idling behind him. So this was where he lived? This was the home of Joey Sternjaw. Not bad, though he would have preferred one of the craftsmen. Stone seemed overly formal to him, and likely to soak up heat in the Southern California sun.

"Don't just stand there," called the cabbie.

McElwee turned to see him licking his fingers, counting a stack of dollar bills.

"Why not?"

"You'll get shot."

"Why would I get shot?"

McElwee had started to walk toward the passenger window, but the cabbie waved him off.

"Stay clear," he said. "I don't want to get caught in the crossfire."

"Why would I get shot?" McElwee asked again.

"You're a private dick, right?"

How did he know that, McElwee wondered? Was Joey Sternjaw such a celebrity in LA that cabbies knew him by sight? Or was this what McElwee's editor liked to call an "information leak," where a character knows something that hasn't yet been revealed to him?

"And?" said McElwee, waiting for the driver to elaborate on the significance of being a private dick.

The cabbie stuffed the wad of ones into his shirt pocket and said, "Those are the rules." Then he hit the gas and peeled away from the curb.

McElwee stood blinking as the cab fled in a cloud of blue smoke. He heard another vehicle approaching from his right. In a second, the staccato of machinegun fire almost burst his eardrums. Bullets whizzed around his head, blasting chunks out of the stone wall behind him. McElwee froze in terror. The car sped up as it passed, raking the sidewalk, the bushes, the walls and trees with gunfire. It passed so close, he could see into the barrel of the fire-breathing Tommy gun. Feet glued to the sidewalk, legs paralyzed with terror, McElwee almost wet himself.

The shooter sprayed the next house, and the blue Chevy slowed in front of it for no apparent reason, then stopped three houses down.

They're coming back, McElwee thought. They're coming to finish me off. Why wouldn't his legs move? Why did his body fail him in this moment of terror? What happened to fight or flight?

The Chevy's transmission made a winding sound as the car backed up. It stopped a few feet in front of him. The rear door opened and all six and a half feet of Polski got out. The

Thompson submachine gun in his right hand pointed at the ground, and he looked annoyed.

Still frozen with fear, McElwee watched him walk to the metal garbage can by the front steps and yank off the lid.

"You're supposed to cover up, you stupid fuck!"

Polski thrust the metal lid into McElwee's hand and said, "Now I'm gonna reload and we're going to do it right this time. Capiche?"

"Why are you shooting at me?"

"I need a motive?"

"Is it because I humiliated you in front of your friends?"

"That'll work. Try to protect yourself this time."

Polski got back in the car. McElwee examined the garbage can lid. The thin galvanized steel might stop an arrow, but not a bullet. He wondered how long it would take Polski to reload the Tommy gun, and whether he'd be better off bolting into the house.

Before he could finish the thought, the blue Chevy approached again from the left.

Impossible, McElwee thought. He can't be coming back because he never even drove away.

Again, the spray of gunfire erupted, and again McElwee was surprised at how loud it was. Polski's red, pocked face was twisted in a sadistic snarl of hatred. The snarl was the work of a writer who wanted to make sure the reader understood who the bad guy was.

McElwee held up the garbage can lid to protect himself. It seemed to attract the bullets like a magnet. He felt the thuds as they hit, he saw sparks fly from the points of impact, and heard the slugs fall to the ground. Nothing came through.

A Tommy gun, he knew from his research, used the same bullets as a Colt 45 pistol. They were powerful enough to penetrate a shield much stronger than a flimsy garbage can lid. In *Extraordinary Joe*, a villain in chapter twenty-seven used a Tommy to shoot through a steel door and wound the main character.

With this thought came another memory. Sitting at a table in a restaurant, the frizzy-haired woman with the big owl eyes had criticized him for that particular scene.

He had protested that it was technically correct. He researched it. Repeated shots from a forty-five-caliber gun would heat and weaken the steel. The first few shots might not go through, but the later ones would if they were hitting the same spot.

"That's not the point," the woman said. "The point is you've stooped to having good guys and bad guys settling things with guns. You used to have actual characters. People with thoughts and feelings and souls, and the solutions to their problems were as complex as the causes."

She was right. That was one of the criticisms that stung.

The Chevy stopped two houses up. Polski poked his head out, smiled, and gave a thumbs-up. McElwee took that to mean he had played his part right.

Then Polski snarled and said, "Consider that a warning, Sternjaw."

A warning, McElwee wondered? A hundred shots from a machine gun in a quiet middle class neighborhood, in broad daylight? That's a warning? Where the hell are the cops in this town?

He waited in front of the house for a few minutes to see if a patrol car arrived. Surely someone would have called the police after that many shots.

Eight minutes went by. Just as he turned to go into the house, an LAPD black-and-white pulled up. No siren, no lights, no urgency. The car had drifted lazily down the street like an ice cream truck in summertime.

McElwee walked to the curb as the roller slowed.

The cop said, "You see a Negro around here wearing a stolen hat?"

"All that gunfire," said McElwee, "and you're worried about a hat?"

"I said Negro."

Well, the author got one thing right, thought McElwee as he watched the car prowl on. He nailed the racial attitude of the 1948 Los Angeles Police Department.

# 10

The door of the house—dark heavy wood that narrowed to a pointed arch at the top—was locked. Though his pants pockets had been empty until now, McElwee had the feeling that if he reached in, he'd find a key. And sure enough, he did.

He was starting to get a sense for this universe, whose author lacked the foresight to lay the groundwork for coming events, instead causing items to magically appear as needed, so the plot could move along. The fact that the key had appeared on demand, and that it fit the lock, told McElwee he was meant to enter.

He listened to the creak as the door swung slowly inward with the key still in the lock. He thought for a second about announcing his presence with a loud Hello, then decided against it. He was unarmed, had no idea who or what was inside, and didn't want to invite another round of gunfire.

After a moment's hesitation, he stepped into the living room. The dark wood floors and dark furniture upholstered in floral patterns were in keeping with the English country style of the house, though they seemed out of character for a tough detective.

Two magazines lay on the coffee table: an architectural review, and a celebrity tabloid open to a spread of photos showing a glamorous couple caught off guard, on what looked like a date they weren't supposed to be having. Perhaps this was a case Joey Sternjaw had been investigating.

Beside the open magazine, a half-empty cup of coffee and a fully empty tumbler whose last drying drop of brown liquid McElwee assumed was whiskey.

Through the broad archway in the rear right wall was a dining room containing one dark heavy wood table large enough to seat six, and two matching chairs. Where were the rest of the chairs? And why were the walls bare? A bachelor such as Sternjaw—McElwee assumed he was a bachelor—may not decorate extravagantly, but surely he wouldn't leave a room in his own home as desolate as this.

No, thought McElwee. The lack of furnishing and decor wasn't Sternjaw's fault. It was the author's. Few scenes were likely to unfold in a detective's dining room, which meant the author had little or no occasion to describe it. And as everything in an author's universe sprang into being at his word, undescribed meant uncreated, and hence, unfurnished. McElwee wondered if Sternjaw had no social life, or didn't care for eating, or if his author simply didn't touch on these matters.

The next room, the kitchen, made his heart sink. It was almost identical to the kitchen in the bare apartment in which he'd woken up that morning. This author, whoever he was, was apparently not capable of dreaming up more than one layout, one set of appliances, one ugly orange and red table. Even the cat food cans beside the sink were the same.

In the fridge, he found a pitcher of orange juice, a quart of milk, half a turkey sandwich, and several bowls of leftovers: chicken with lemon and pepper, mashed potatoes, green beans. Someone in the house cooked.

He walked back through the living room, around the wood stairway, to the rear study. Sternjaw's unpaid bills lay on an open rolltop desk in front of a wooden swivel chair. He was two months behind on the phone and electric, three on water.

Why then did he own a Mont Blanc fountain pen? McElwee picked it up from the desk and admired its heft. Perhaps it was a gift from a client.

Two maps were mounted on the wall behind him: one of West Hollywood, the other of greater Los Angeles. Both had blank spots. These must be places Sternjaw had not yet visited; otherwise, the author would have filled them in.

On the rear wall, a window looked out onto the backyard, where neglected foot-tall grass luxuriated in the shade of a sprawling magnolia. McElwee had never stopped to think who mowed the lawns of private detectives in 1940s crime novels, so he couldn't fault Sternjaw's author for that oversight.

Back to the living room and up the stairs. The second floor was smaller, darker. The door on the left of the short hallway led to a bathroom. He stepped in to get a look at the sink and toilet, medicine chest with uncracked mirror, metal claw-foot tub. The clear plastic shower curtain was an anachronism. McElwee was pretty sure those didn't exist in 1948.

Why would the author have put it there? So whoever was in the shower could see his attacker coming. McElwee removed his notebook from his pocket and wrote "Careful in bathroom."

Sliding the notebook back into his pocket, he made one final mental note. The bathroom's dark wood trim broke the tyranny of white tiled walls and floor, giving this room a more homey, less institutional look than the one in this morning's apartment.

Across from the bathroom, a closed door. A closet. It was tiny. Four hanging suits, an iron, and an ironing board. As a PI, Sternjaw would have to appear in court now and then. Hence the suits. He probably ironed his own shirts to save money.

Last door on the second floor, the bedroom. He pushed the door open. Dark wood floor, dark wood bed sheeted in white.

"Was that you getting shot out there?"

My God, McElwee thought, this author makes beautiful women.

The one who had posed the question was thin and lithe, with arrow-straight posture. She sat on the edge of the bed in a white robe. Wisps of hair escaped the dyed blonde bun behind her head as she turned to face him. Her bright blue eyes, rimmed red from crying, conveyed warmth and intelligence in equal measure. In the grace of that simple movement, the turn of her head on that long slim neck, he saw a beauty he had never been able to capture on the page, however hard he had tried.

For the first time, he felt a pang of jealousy. The author of this half-assed universe might have created a character more compelling than his own.

Shake it off, he told himself. It's just a crush. And you know how those turn out. Let's stick to business and try to figure out what the hell's going on here.

"Dorothy?" he guessed.

"I suppose you've heard by now?"

"About Lady Astor?"

"Please, call her Agatha. Or Gram."

She stood and kissed him, and then put her arms around him.

"I hate the idea of people shooting at you," she said into his shoulder. "Why can't you be a teacher or an architect?"

Her body was so lean, he could feel her ribs when they hugged. The flesh of her arms and back was firm and toned. He guessed she was around his age, Joey Sternjaw's age, thirty or so.

"Where were you last night?" she asked. Both her question and her tone made him nervous.

"I don't know."

She drew her head away and looked him in the eye.

"You don't know?"

McElwee stole a glance at the diamond ring on her left hand. Was she his wife?

He rubbed his left thumb against his own ring finger. Nothing there. But did men wear wedding rings in the '40s? Or did that tradition start later?

"I called," Dorothy said, letting go of him and turning back toward the bed. "After I found Gram. Did you know I was the one who found her? It was awful, Joey. Awful!"

He looked again at her hand and saw there were two rings. Engagement and wedding. Platinum or white gold. The diamond looked too big and bright for a private investigator's salary.

Was she his mistress?

She caught him looking at the ring. "Oh, don't worry about him," she said. "He doesn't even know I'm gone. And if he did, he wouldn't care."

Mistress, thought McElwee, with mixed emotions. He had been married for two years in real life. His wife, Leanne, had been a drunk, just like him. Alcohol had held them together, and alcohol had driven them apart. They both sobered up after the divorce and realized they hated each other.

Now she wrote romance novels. Bad ones, McElwee liked to tell himself, but they outsold his early literary works a hundred to one. It irked him to see himself so clearly in all her villains. It irked him that her books even had villains. They didn't belong in the romance genre, but she had always found more fulfillment in hating her enemies than in loving her friends.

His ex couldn't conceive of a world without someone to despise, so her romances had bad guys. When her editor suggested she might be better off writing thrillers—a genre that naturally lent itself to the battle of good and evil—she wrote him into a Regency as an illiterate footman and had him trampled to death beneath a coach and six.

McElwee had vowed never to marry again, but over the past year, he'd been rethinking that. I'm getting older, he told himself, and I don't want to die alone. But I'm not going back into the dog crate yet. Maybe when I'm fifty, if anyone still likes me.

Score one for not being married, he thought, looking at Dorothy. And negative one for having to share this lovely woman with another man.

"I called the police," said Dorothy. "And then I called you. But you didn't answer, so I came over and let myself in. I thought maybe Frump had already gotten ahold of you. Maybe you were already on the case."

"Frump?"

"It's funny," she said. "He'd been at the house earlier in the evening. Gram was very fond of him."

"Of Frump? Who could be fond of him?" Certainly not the rich old dowager the newspaper had described. Agatha Astor sounded like a stuffy old snoot, obsessed with social status, old money, and family pedigree.

Dorothy shrugged. "Does anything make sense in this world? Anyway, Frump was the one who responded to the call. I showed him the body and the safe, and then I had to leave. I just couldn't be there, in that house, after all that had happened. I wanted *you*. You've been my sanity these past few months."

How was he supposed to respond to that? Women didn't talk to him that way. The nicest thing Leanne ever said was, "I'll let you do that again after you empty the dishwasher and take out the trash."

Dorothy didn't fit the mold of whatever universe he had fallen into. Clear-eyed, graceful, eloquent, and open-hearted, her praise was both generous and genuine. McElwee felt a deep empathy for this woman who was clearly devoted to a man who probably didn't deserve her, a two-dimensional crime solver and second-rate Raymond Chandler knockoff.

He grasped at once that her road had been and would continue to be a hard one. The world she'd been born into was neither rich enough nor deep enough to accommodate a person of true feeling who could utter thoughtful sentences. Lovely Dorothy, deep and unfulfilled...

Stop it, he commanded himself. You're crushing again. And authoring, casting her into a story before you even know who she is. You're a detective, Joe, whether you want to be or not. You should be gathering facts, not spinning fantasies.

"Are you thinking?" The surprise in Dorothy's eyes told him this was something new and unexpected. "Please tell me you are!"

She practically lunged at him, alighting just before collision with a soft hand on his shoulder.

"Yeah. I was thinking, if you wanted comfort, why didn't you go to..."

He let the question hang, hoping she'd fill in her husband's name.

"Walter? Don't be absurd!"

Walter, eh? Sounds like an insensitive brute.

"And where was Walter when all this went down?"

The hesitation in her eyes told him he'd hit a sore spot.

"You know I don't talk about those sorts of things. Now I'm going to ask you one last time. Where were you last night?"

She tilted her head back and pushed her chin out when she was angry. The girlish gesture of defiance accentuated the sharp line of her jaw. Her confrontational posture and tone reminded him of Leanne. How many times had his ex asked him that very question? And how many times had he responded with the only answer he could give now?

"I don't know."

Dorothy's manner was softer than Leanne's. Where Leanne and Joseph McElwee had been partners in masochistic misery, twisting the knife of betrayal into each other and themselves, this woman so clearly loved Joey Sternjaw that McElwee felt awful about letting her down.

"Well I do." She turned and picked up a piece of paper from the nightstand.

Her eyes were tearing as she handed it to him.

He unfolded and read the note, written in a looping woman's hand.

"Come see me."

It was signed with a big red kiss.

"Who left this?" McElwee asked.

"Are you telling me you don't know?"

He had an idea. The woman in green from the diner. Who else but a brazen femme fatale would hand a note like that to a man's mistress?

"Do you think I'm stupid, Joey? A handsome man like you with a job that keeps him out all hours of the night? Even if you are a runt, you have your charms. And at the end of the day, you *are* a man."

For a moment, McElwee thought that was a compliment. As in, maybe I'm not the biggest guy in the world, but I *am* a man. Then it clicked. "Man" was a synonym for slut, for opportunists who fell into bed with whoever would have them.

"Did she come by here?" he asked.

"Obviously, if she left the note."

"What was she wearing?" McElwee wanted to make sure it was the same woman he had seen in the diner that morning.

"Not much," Dorothy said with contempt. "But who can blame her? I can't imagine where she'd find a dress large enough to contain those swollen udders."

That's her, McElwee thought. But how was he supposed to visit her if he didn't know where she lived? He didn't even know her name, for God's sake.

If he had written this scene, he would have put a phone number on the note and skipped the big red kiss, which was over the top. However pretty the women in this world were, the exposition sucked. He was beginning to think he knew who the author was. A perennial bestseller whom he particularly disliked.

If he was right, this scene would end with some clunky device containing just enough information to get him to the next chapter.

"Oh," said Dorothy, "and here's her card."

11

Veronica Mayweather, voluptuous caricature of female sexuality, lived just two blocks down and around the corner.

McElwee cursed the whole way there. He should have put it together earlier. If the cartoonish opening scene, the poorly described apartment, the unprovoked attacks from the snarling Polski—if none of those tropes had tipped him off, he should have known the second he saw Veronica's colossal breasts that he was in the Turnerverse.

Niall Turner, with his impossible plots, gratuitous sex, timelines that went in circles, thousand-round shootouts where the hero never got hit, characters who couldn't stay in character, and worlds in which the laws of physics changed from chapter to chapter to accommodate the action—Niall Turner was McElwee's least favorite author.

Turner's standalone novels exceeded the stupidity of even his Bronco Howitzer series, a feat McElwee had considered impossible until he read a few of them.

Turner had committed every offense in the mystery writer's playbook. Who was the culprit in his most famous whodunnit? The detective himself. A cardinal no-no. How did the serial killer continue to kill even after the cops had locked him in a cell with his identical twin, who was also a serial killer? It was the identical triplet!

That book, panned by critics and thinking readers everywhere, sold four million copies and spawned a sequel with a long-lost identical-quadruplet-serial-killer who was somehow even more evil and two-dimensional than his siblings.

McElwee tried to tell himself that people read that dreck just to mock its awfulness, like watching movies that were so unintentionally bad they made you laugh.

But no! According to the reviews on Amazon and Goodreads, people actually enjoyed Turner's stories. They praised the innovative twists you could never see coming.

Well of course you can't see them coming, McElwee thought. Because it's impossible to blow up a house with a single can of Lysol. It's impossible for the hero's final bullet to ricochet off six steel walls and kill all six villains in the final showdown.

"I fucking hate that guy," he said aloud as he pounded his fist on Veronica Mayweather's front door.

The door swung open right away. The buxom redhead standing behind it let the black silk robe fall from her shoulders, cupped one enormous breast in each hand and said with wonder and delight, "Can you believe the size of these things?"

"Jesus Christ!" said McElwee, pushing past her. "He panders to the lowest common denominator. That's why so many people read him. He exaggerates everything, so even the dumbest reader gets it! Put your clothes on!"

"And look at this," Veronica said. She untied the silk belt that had kept her robe from falling below her waist, then ran her fingers through the copper red triangle between her thighs. "I'm a *real* redhead," she giggled.

When she turned and shut the door, McElwee did everything in his power not to look at her. He would never succumb to Turner's cheap thrills, his improbable setups and poorly drawn characters. But God, Turner did have a good sense of *what* to exaggerate.

So what, McElwee thought, as he tried his best to pry his eyes from her voluptuous body. I won't give in. I won't. What does Turner think, that I'm just a bundle of animal impulses?

In bed half an hour later, he lay staring at the ceiling, justifying his lapse with a quiet internal dialogue.

Seriously, he thought, how many times in your life do you even *see* a woman like this, much less get to sleep with her? And doesn't a writer have a responsibility to experience everything, so he can convey the world as richly as possible to his readers?

An image popped into his head of Frump naked in the bed beside him. Ok, he thought with a wince, maybe not *everything*. But everything a reader would like to fantasize about.

This thought troubled him. If it was right, if shallow wish-fulfillment was all readers wanted, then Turner was right to create the crappy thrill-a-minute fantasies his audiences devoured.

McElwee turned to look at the woman he vowed never to see again. She was lighting a cigarette.

"Who knew I'd like these things?" she said, blowing a cloud of smoke toward the ceiling. "In real life, they're disgusting. But in all the old movies Turner watches to get his ideas—"

She turned and gave him a serious look. "You know he doesn't read, don't you? He gets all his ideas from film and television."

"I know," McElwee said.

"He's on a classic film kick now, and in old movies, smoking was glamorous. It had no consequences. Look." She kissed his mouth then drew back to watch his reaction. "No ashtray breath, see?"

"That *is* odd," McElwee admitted.

"No, it's not. It's actually one of the keys to understanding the Turnerverse. There are no consequences. They're too complex for him to handle, so he omits them. You know, in real life, when someone gets killed, it tears the social fabric. It leaves this horrible bleeding hole in people's hearts, and they grieve. But in the Turnerverse, killing is just a setup for revenge. And, as for physical consequences, did you know one of his protagonists ran six blocks after being shot eleven times in both legs?

"No one can run six blocks with twenty-two bullets in their legs. But that doesn't matter to Turner. The point is to constantly ratchet up the tension and the stakes. If one bullet puts the reader on edge, then twenty-two should really make him sweat. And I do mean him. Turner writes for men."

She doesn't talk like a femme fatale, McElwee thought. She's actually quite thoughtful. He decided she wasn't a Turner creation.

"Come to think of it," she said, "that was you with the gunshot wounds. Joey Sternjaw, book four. Remember?"

"No. I stopped reading Turner years ago. The only reason I read him in the first place was to understand what writers *shouldn't* do. I studied him the way structural engineers study failed bridges."

"And yet he rakes in millions every year. Your last literary work sold, what? A hundred and eighty copies?"

"How did you know that?"

"You told me a few months ago, when you came for dinner. Remember?"

Now it came back him. The bookstore signing, in... in whatever that rinky-dink Virginia town was. It took him two hours to drive there. He'd visited in the summer, just before *Extraordinary Joe* hit the market, to have dinner with Veronica. But her last name was Wentworth, not Mayweather. Veronica with the black frizzy hair and owl-eyes, the astute reader with the dead-on critique.

"You're selling out," she had told him over dinner at the Indian restaurant.

She had received an advance copy, and though she promised to give him a reading to promote it, she made no effort to hide her contempt for the book.

"Don't knock it," he said. "I think it has mass-market appeal. If it takes off, well, it's books like that that keep your store in business."

"Books like that keep me afloat so I can sell books like you used to write. That's the whole reason I went into this line of work in the first place. You were once the bright star. Now you're the necessary evil."

"Who cares how bright a star is if there's no one there to see it?"

He tried to steer the conversation back to his earlier works. He liked the way she praised them. They seemed to evoke a tenderness in her. He thought he might get laid and not have to drive back home till the next morning.

But she wouldn't let him off the hook.

"You have Turner envy," she told him.

"No, I don't!"

"Your new book reads just like one of his."

"No way."

"Way," she said. "Your characters are thin, your plot is far-fetched. You're like a washed-up rock band. They can't make interesting music anymore, so they keep turning up the volume. You're just dialing it in, Joe."

"Turner's been dialing it in for thirty years." He disliked his defensive tone. It sounded like an admission that he was, in fact, dialing it in.

"And he's been making bank," Veronica said. "That's why you envy him."

"I don't envy him. He writes garbage. He's a sellout."

"He never had the talent to sell out. He's as shallow as his novels. But you! You sold out. You couldn't stand that everyone in the country knew his name. He sells to a big audience that's easy to please, so you decided to go after that audience yourself."

"I am not Niall Turner," he insisted. His tone made clear she had insulted him.

"No, you're not. You're actually a lot better than him. Or you were. Your ego got the better of you, and your insecurities, and your greed, and you dumbed down a great talent to cater to readers with shallow minds and deep pockets. Readers you don't even like.

"You're missing your calling, Joe. You have more wit and insight than Turner ever had. Your sentences are better. The audience for what you do is smaller and they have a smaller pool of work to choose from. Thinking minds need to be fed by thinking minds. We can't afford to lose one like you. Don't abandon us, Joe!"

McElwee emerged from his memory to the sight of Veronica Mayweather's big green eyes. She lay beside him, head propped on her hand, long copper-red hair flowing over painted nails.

"Wait," he said. "You're the bookstore manager. You're..."

"Veronica. Same name there as here. Only here, I'm a Turner girl." She smiled—straight, white, movie-star teeth framed by lips whose lipstick didn't smear even during the clumsiest sex.

And it *had* been clumsy. She was bigger than him. He had felt like an overexcited high school boy wrestling with a stronger opponent who laughed a lot. He felt he'd made a bad impression.

"The trick to enjoying Turner," Veronica said, "is the same as the trick to enjoying ice cream and sex and roller coasters."

"What's that?"

"Just let go. Give in. Surrender."

Feeling slightly humiliated by his lackluster performance and by the fact that he hadn't been able to resist the creation of an author he despised, he blurted, "To this dreck? Never!"

She sat up. "Tell me, Joe, which do you like better? The intellectual and aesthetic superiority of the literature you claim to create, or these." She shoved her oversized boobs in his face.

While the half of him above the sheets tried to appear indifferent, the part below sprang to life with raging enthusiasm. Once again, McElwee found himself losing to Turner.

He surrendered with a shrug. "In for a penny, in for a pound."

# 12

Exhaling the first puff of her post-round-two cigarette, Veronica told him she had always wanted to experience the vaunted sexual prowess of Turner's Joey Sternjaw.

Joey was one of Turner's more recent creations, a rare character with backstory and vulnerability. Veronica explained that Sternjaw was the youngest son of a New Jersey longshoreman who belittled him for being the runt of the litter.

"Your daddy used to put you in a white dress and pour beer on your head. Then he and your brothers would kick you down the stairs, where your sister would secretly gather you up and take you into her bed and comfort you."

"That's my backstory? That's the best Turner could do?"

Veronica nodded. "The point is supposed to be that little Joey Sternjaw has a heart because he understands what it's like to be picked on. He toughened up and learned to fight, and every Joey Sternjaw book has a chapter where the bad guys underestimate him because of his small stature, and he teaches them a lesson. When Turner omitted that episode from book six of the series, his readers were up in arms. So in book seven, he beat up two big guys. That fellow you slugged in front of the diner this morning—"

"Polski," McElwee said.

"Is that his name?"

"Yes."

"Oh, God." She rolled her eyes. "And I bet he's Polish."

"Sure enough!"

"Well, that was the obligatory Sternjaw-shows-'em chapter, and I must admit I was proud of you. But the whole confrontation was poorly set up. I mean, what motive did they have for just rolling up like that and picking a fight?"

McElwee shrugged.

"Anyway," Veronica said, "don't get me started unpacking Joey's backstory. Putting a boy in a dress, humiliating him, and then sending him to his sister's bed for comfort..."

"You know, Turner's more astute readers have known for decades about his sexual issues. Take you, for example."

"I'm a Turner sexual issue?"

"The walking, talking embodiment. Supposedly your small stature is less threatening, more vulnerable, easier to love. You're not just some overpowering brute. Turner says you're in touch with your sensitive side. He even sometimes calls it your feminine side, and I'll excuse for a moment his confusion of those two things. But that's the problem. He keeps *saying* it, but he never shows it.

"Now you're also good in bed, according to Turner anyway. I can't vouch for that because it's over too soon for me to get a real taste.

"But what is Turner's idea of 'good in bed'? Well, it isn't pillow talk, and it isn't a lingering caress. It isn't playfulness or tenderness or emotional connection. It's... Well, you're five foot three—"

"I'm five-six!" McElwee blurted.

"Whatever. And that thing between your legs belongs to a man seven feet tall."

"I noticed that when I was showering."

"What does it tell you about a writer when he equates 'good in bed' with just being big? It tells me the same thing the rest of his writing tells me, which is that he doesn't understand anything at all."

"Except how to sell books."

"Except that. Right. How to sell books to men. Oh, and the other thing about Sternjaw, he can have sex thirty times in one day—"

"He can?"

"Supposedly," she said. "But I don't see what's so attractive about that. The thought of it makes me sore. Are you hungry?"

He was.

"So am I," Veronica said. "But I want one more crack at you before we eat. I haven't been getting my money's worth from you, and I want to wring every ounce of pleasure from this body in the short time I have it."

"So do I!"

His tone was too enthusiastic. Hers was playful. "Perv!"

She rolled on top of him and they began round three.

<h1 align="center">13</h1>

"This place looks exactly like the diner from this morning," McElwee said. "But we're in a different neighborhood."

He and Veronica sat in the corner booth she alone had occupied that morning. Her dress, now purple satin, was cut more modestly than the green dress in which she had first appeared.

"I know," she said. "You ever see those old cartoons where the characters keep running past the same things, like the background is just a loop that repeats every couple of seconds? That's how Turner writes his settings. In fact, he doesn't even write them himself anymore."

"How do you know that?"

"My friend works for his publisher in New York. You know how the bylines on all his books now say, Niall Turner with such-and-such co-author? He gets the co-authors to crank out all the parts he doesn't feel like writing. Settings, characterization, sometimes dialogue, because he's so bad at it."

"Then what's left for him to write?"

"Sex, action, and gore. The protagonist's snappy comebacks that let you know he's not to be trifled with. Oh, and the plot twists. The ones you can't see coming because they make no sense."

To the waitress, she said, "I'll have a BLT and a cup of coffee. Cream, no sugar."

"Ditto," said McElwee, "but hold the bacon."

"Poor girl," Veronica said as the waitress walked away.

"Why poor? What's wrong with her?"

"Young, pretty, face full of promise. Her throat will be slit before the day's out."

"That's a terrible thing to say!"

"Why do you think she's dressed all in white?" Veronica asked. "Turner likes the blood to show."

"You really think he'll kill her?"

"Come on, Joe. Women have only two roles in Turner's fiction: to get killed by the bad guy or screwed by the good guy. I guess I got the better of the two options, but not by much. You have *got* to up your game! Sex is the whole body, the mind and spirit and heart. It's anticipation and mystery and surprise, and I'm not getting any of that from you."

"I can only work with what I've got."

"And in the Turnerverse, that isn't much. You have to bring Joe McElwee into the game. Your early books had such heart! So much feeling, and such a deep understanding of human nature!"

"And a world of good they did me."

"I'll let you in on a little secret."

"What?"

"I always fantasized about sleeping with Joe McElwee."

"Really?"

She nodded. "And you wanted to fuck me too."

"What? When?"

"Last summer, at dinner in the Indian restaurant. Oh, come on, Joe! You think I couldn't read your look? I know exactly what you were thinking."

McElwee felt a tinge of discomfort, but he also thought she was bluffing. She couldn't have known what he was thinking. If he called her out, she would say the wrong thing. Her interpretation of what he'd been thinking would simply be a projection of her own thoughts. He decided to challenge her.

"What was I thinking?" McElwee asked.

"You liked the praise I heaped on your early work. I could see your ego swell. You were thinking I wasn't very pretty and probably didn't have many opportunities with men, and because I said nice things about you, you'd have an easy time getting me into bed. You were calculating how long the drive home would take the next day, and whether you'd have to stick around for breakfast."

"Holy crap!" McElwee felt even more exposed than he had expected.

"It's the same thing with every guy. And to be honest, I've finally accepted it. I'm forty-one. I'm not looking for a fairytale romance. I'm not looking for marriage. I lived with a guy for three years, and that was enough. I *do* like to be loved, and I also like to be done with being loved.

"The fact that I'm not pretty—I used to resent that. I can't tell you how much energy I wasted lamenting my looks, trying to be someone I wasn't. You know what guys are like with a not-very-pretty woman? They're honest and real. They don't put up a front. They're not trying to lure me in with false promises because I'm not the big prize, I'm not worth a big campaign.

"I can see the calculations in their eyes. I know the moment they start to think they can score, and it's never at the beginning of the conversation. Guys don't approach me to hit on me. They approach me because they want to know where a book is, or whether I'm in line to order coffee.

"It starts as a practical conversation, an information exchange. And then there's the click. 'She's talking to me. I bet she doesn't get a lot of attention. I could do her a favor.'"

McElwee put his head in his hands, embarrassed. "This is painful."

"No it's not. Because then the decision is mine. Maybe I want to see what this guy is like. Sex for me is like reading. Every man is a different book. Sometimes I'm disappointed, sometimes I'm surprised. No way am I going to limit myself to just one, just like there's no way I'd limit myself to a single author. They all have something different to show me.

"And because I'm not worth the effort of building some grand facade, what the guys show me is their real selves. The good, the bad, and the ugly. Good sex has all that rolled in. Good literature too. You went and turned your back on that, and that's why I brought you here. To rub your nose in the Turnerverse so you can see what you're becoming.

"Also, I wanted to see what I'd become." She looked down at her big chest and frowned. "It's pretty much what I expected. The fantasy of a middle-school boy."

"How do you like being a caricature?"

The waitress returned, poured two cups of coffee, and left a small pitcher of cream on the table.

"Lean in, I say." Veronica poured cream in her coffee and then into McElwee's. "I'm going whole hog on the femme fatale bit because, why not? Remember, there are no consequences in the Turnerverse. What happens in Vegas stays in Vegas.

"The whole reason I read is to live in someone else's skin for a while, and Veronica Mayweather has some damn nice skin. I'll tell you something though. I wouldn't want to look like this all the time. I mean, I love the way it turns you on. Nothing turns me on more than seeing how much I turn my lover on.

"But there's a time and a place for that, and the rest of the time, I don't want to be looked at that way. I went to the grocer's this morning to buy some peaches. Thirteen-year-old boys and sixty-year-old men all stared at me the same way, like I was built for one thing.

"That's a flaw not just in Turner's men, but in the race in general. Whoever made our universe, the real one that you and I came from, overdid it on the spreading-your-seed thing. I mean, I know we have to survive in a competitive world, and sure, men's always-on sex drive helps replenish the species faster than death can deplete it, but I'd like to be able to buy some peaches without a bunch of pervs staring a hole in my ass. How's your coffee?"

"Weak."

"Figures."

"About the grocery store," McElwee said. "That dress you had on—don't you think that played a part in how people looked at you?"

"It wasn't my choice. In the Turnerverse, if a woman has boobs, they're on display. You should see what's in my closet. It's practically a stripper's wardrobe. You know what, though? The looks I got from the women in the store were worse than the ones from the men. So judgmental! Who the hell are they to look at me like that? When I'm buying fucking peaches! They don't *know* me.

"But it was a wakeup call, because I do the same thing. There's this woman who comes into the bookstore every few weeks. She wears spandex and buys books about exercise and fruit smoothies. Has perfectly flat abs. I hate her, but I'm going to try not to. I'm going to try to remind myself what it's like to be on the receiving end of that judgmental look."

When the waitress put their sandwiches down, Veronica looked from the young woman's nametag to her wrist and seemed to startle. In a lightning-quick movement, she dumped her coffee onto the young woman's uniform. Suzette, if the nametag was correct, shrieked as if burned and jumped back, pawing at the brown liquid, inadvertently rubbing it further into the white fabric.

"What is wrong with you?" she cried.

The other customers were looking over at them now.

"Listen, hon," said Veronica, "go home and change out of that uniform. Put on something dark that doesn't show blood."

"What? I have a—"

"Date after work. I know. He's a psychopath. You go home and change, and stay around people you know tonight. Be with at least two other people at all times, and make sure neither one of them is that date of yours."

The waitress stood there blinking stupidly. "How did you know I had a date?"

Veronica put her hand on the young woman's shoulder. "Go tell your boss you're taking the rest of the day off. Go home, change your clothes, stay with people you know, and avoid Romeo."

The directness and sincerity of her speech convinced the girl. She turned, went to the counter, and told her boss she was leaving.

The customers who had been watching turned back to their meals.

"How did you know that?" McElwee asked. "That she had a date?"

"I'll tell you later," Veronica said. "I just gave him writer's block."

"Who?"

"Turner. If his characters don't conform to the plot, he doesn't know what to do. A good author— Well, you know that famous quote from Tolstoy about Anna Karenina? She was supposed to marry Vronsky, but it turned out she didn't want to. Tolstoy spent years writing that book, getting everything in place so Anna could marry her beau. When she said no, the author was flabbergasted. His own character had gotten away from him.

"So what did he do? He rolled with it. Anna was so well drawn, she'd become alive. She made her own choices, and the author sacrificed his plot to let her be herself. That's good writing. Tolstoy had the courage to let his creation lead, and she's still alive today, even though she offed herself.

"Turner can't create anything at that level. He doesn't even try because he sees his job as something different. He needs an explosion in chapter one, a sex scene in chapter six, a shootout in twelve, potential failure of the entire operation in chapter twenty-two, and a happy ending in thirty-six.

"It's the same kind of crap you're writing, Joe. You have better descriptive skills, and a decent ear for dialogue, but the old Joe who would have let his living, breathing Anna die now has her turn to cardboard and marry Vronsky. Why, Joe? Because your audience research tells you happy endings sell?

"You have Turner envy, and it leaves me cold. Even in bed, you leave me cold, and that's a shame, because I know the spark is still in you. I'm going to rattle you until I get it out. Seriously, Joe, all I'm looking for is a good romp. A few hours out of my own skin and my own workaday life and into a world done right.”

“Wait, are you talking about sex or reading?”

“Both.”

# 14

McElwee returned to his house at 123 Terra under the dusky twilight of a warm June evening. The smog that had settled over the city obscured the dimmer stars overhead, while Venus glowed brightly in the purpling west.

What's missing, he asked himself as he made his way up the front steps. Turning his key in the lock, he heard the click and thought, planes. Jets fly in and out of LAX every minute, but passenger jets don't exist yet. Flying is too expensive for the masses. It's actually kind of nice to be in a city this size without all those crisscross lines in the sky. Without the noise of jets taking off and landing.

"Hello, Joey."

He stopped just inside the door. He had forgotten about Dorothy. She had risen from the couch as she spoke, as if she'd been waiting for him.

"I'm sorry about this morning," she said.

Sorry? He was the one who felt sorry. More so now that he had actually committed the infidelity she had earlier accused him of. But, he wondered, could he really be unfaithful to a woman he technically didn't even know? To a woman he hadn't slept with and, in fact, hadn't even met until a few hours ago?

He decided it was best not to split hairs. If she felt betrayed, the wound was real.

"It isn't fair of me to ask fidelity of you when I'm married to someone else," Dorothy said. "Even if the marriage is a sham."

A sham? Maybe Joey Sternjaw wasn't sharing Dorothy with anyone. Maybe he had her, body and soul, all to himself. For a second, that buoyed his spirits. Then it depressed him. If she was exclusive to him, he should be to her. And yet, she was so generous, she didn't begrudge an unmarried man his escapades.

She should have. He made a note to talk to her about that, about the line between kindness and understanding on the one hand and being a doormat on the other.

She kissed him and told him dinner was waiting in the dining room.

What was this? A mistress who came to his house and cooked? Turner did that sort of thing to women, made them serve all a man's appetites.

"You cooked?"

"Oh, Joey, you know I can't cook. The kitchen staff at Gram's prepared this. I had the driver bring it over."

It was quite a spread. Veal, the cruelest of meats, which McElwee avoided on principle even back in the days when he regularly ate meat. Mashed potatoes, green beans, pearl onions, fresh baked rolls, champagne, and banana cream pie.

He noted she had moved the chairs from opposite ends of the table to opposite sides. They would sit three feet apart instead of eight feet apart.

He pulled a chair for her and she sat.

He twisted the cork from the champagne bottle, filled her glass, then his. If Veronica could smoke in the Turnerverse without getting bad breath, he could have a glass of champagne without relapsing. There was something to be said for this lack of consequences. He took his seat across from Dorothy and watched her fill her plate. Mashed potatoes, green beans, one roll.

He put the same on his plate, doubling her portions. She was slim and he was... Oh yeah. He was one hundred forty pounds now, not two hundred.

"No veal?" she asked.

"I don't eat meat," he said, forgetting he had eaten it for breakfast. "And even when I did, I wouldn't eat that. It's inhuman, what they do to those calves."

She gave him a strange look. "What a funny thing to say."

"What's funny about it?"

"You've always loved veal. It's your favorite. That's why I asked the cook to make it."

McElwee shook his head. "Not anymore. Sorry."

She smiled. "Well, don't be sorry. To be honest, I feel the same way about the cruelty of it. I never liked that you ate it, and..." She hesitated.

"What," McElwee asked through a mouthful of potatoes.

"Well it used to bother me when you ordered it, because you saw I wouldn't touch it and you never asked why. I hoped one day you'd get the clue and not eat it in front of me."

"Why didn't you say something?"

"What would I have said?"

"Don't eat that stuff, Joey. I don't like it."

"That's hardly the kind of thing a woman in my position is raised to say, especially to a man."

What were you raised to say, if not your actual thoughts? McElwee did the math. If Dorothy was thirty, she would have been born around 1918. She came from a rich family and, judging by her perfect posture, perfect manners, and clear diction, had probably gone to finishing school. No, he thought. She wasn't raised to speak her mind. She was raised to please.

"You can say whatever you want to me," he told her.

"Sure I can." Her dismissive tone made clear she didn't believe him.

He shrugged. "Any news on Gram?"

"Detective Frump has been pounding the pavement, as he puts it. He says he has some clues."

"Any solid leads?"

"Yes, one."

"What's that?" McElwee stuffed too many green beans into his mouth at once. He was conscious of Dorothy watching him eat. He imagined her dining in a mansion, at a giant table with seven forks and seven spoons, different knives for every course, and servants hovering over her. There were guests every night. Her crowd ate slowly, exchanging witty banter between courses, and he was a billy goat with fat green whiskers sticking out of his mouth.

He interpreted her smile as mockery. Leanne used to smile at him like that when his occasional clumsiness confirmed her assessment of his inferiority.

Then Dorothy's smile broke broad and warm, and he chastised himself for being so jaded, for assuming ill will and unkind thoughts in a person who had never shown an ounce of either toward him.

"You know, at home," she said, "we're so bored with all our riches that no one's ever really hungry. It's nice to see you eat with real appetite."

"You should eat too. Go on. And what's this lead?"

"You know how peculiar Gram was."

"Sure," McElwee lied and stuffed another forkful of green beans into his mouth.

"And particular. She was very particular. Well, she had written down the serial numbers on every bill in her safe, three pages worth, front and back in her cramped little hand, and she stuffed those pages into one of the books in the library. Walter found it late this morning. It's the first useful thing he's ever done. And do you know what? Someone spent one of those bills today down on Murder Row. Frump matched the serial number. I'd say that's a solid lead."

Green beans caught in McElwee's throat as he remembered handing the shopkeeper a twenty that morning when he'd purchased the notebook and pencil.

"What is it, Joey? Are you choking?"

She leapt from her seat to help him, but he waved her down.

"I'm fine," he coughed. "I just..." He wiped his chin and took a sip of champagne. "Just food going down the wrong pipe, that's all."

He'd given the man a twenty for a six-cent purchase. That would stick out in 1948. Maybe the old man reported him. Most of the twenties in McElwee's wallet had come from the pile on the floor, though one was his own. He had no way of knowing right now whether he paid with his own money or one of Agatha Astor's registered bills. If it was the latter, and if the shopkeeper could describe him, McElwee's arrest might be imminent.

"When did you last talk to Frump?" he asked.

"An hour ago. He came by."

"And he told you then about the bill?"

"Yes."

McElwee decided he was safe. If Frump had traced the bill back to him, if Frump thought he had killed Agatha Astor, he would not have left her granddaughter alone in the murderer's house. He was pretty sure Dorothy was Lady Astor's granddaughter, given that she kept calling the old woman "Gram."

He wanted to know more about Walter and the marriage, but he wasn't sure how to broach the subject.

"You don't mind if I stay, do you, Joey? I don't want to go home tonight. Gram is dead and Walter is... Well," she said acidly, "you *know* what Walter does."

"Stay the month," McElwee said. And he meant it. Dorothy brought warmth and spirit to a home that was otherwise just a place to shower and sleep.

"I would, if it didn't raise suspicion. What was stolen from the safe was a trifle in the overall scheme of Gram's estate. Walter and I being heirs gives us each a motive to get rid of her. You know how vicious gossip can be in this town. It's best if we keep up appearances until the murderer is caught."

Appearances, he understood, meant not being seen going into and out of your lover's house. The rich lived how they wanted to live, and they did it discreetly. He assumed she'd make her getaway before dawn.

# 15

McElwee lingered in the shower after dinner. He soaped his body twice, trying to wash out every trace of the Turnerverse. Sleeping with Veronica, as much as he had enjoyed it, left him feeling dirty and slightly ashamed. It was the same feeling he'd had after reading the one early Turner novel he'd secretly enjoyed, the same feeling of regret and self-loathing he had in his thirties after a night of drinking too much, or more recently, after eating an entire tub of ice cream that he didn't even like. That appalling feeling of bitter disappointment that asked, how could I give in to that?

The man who succumbed to such temptation wasn't worthy of sharing a bed with Dorothy Astor. At dinner, he'd been looking forward to lying beside her. Now he was looking for excuses not to. What was the word Jean had used this morning, the waitress in the diner on Murder Row who had handed him the newspaper?

Recuse. That was it. She asked if he would have to recuse himself from the case due to his ties to Dorothy and the Astor family. Now, he shut his eyes, soaped his face for the third time, and pictured himself walking into the bedroom after his shower.

She would be on the bed in her gown awaiting him. And he'd say, "I'm sorry, sweetie. I have to recuse myself this evening. I'm not fit to be near you after the day I've had." He didn't want the Turnerverse rubbing off on her. He would sleep on the couch downstairs.

He rinsed and cut the water, found a towel, and opened the window to let out the steam. The walls dripped with moisture. Even the pajamas he'd left by the sink were damp with condensation. He felt like his grandfather as he put them on, the old-fashioned square-cut pants and top, pearl white, with faint red and orange pinstripes. They were surprisingly comfortable. No wonder people slept in them. And they were cotton. In 1948, polyester hadn't yet weaseled its way into every item of a man's wardrobe.

In the bedroom, he found her sitting on the edge of the bed, reading. He wondered if she had been born with perfect posture or had practiced it. It looked natural, and compared to the slackness he'd observed in so many people, her upright bearing conferred an air of nobility. The more he saw of her, the more he felt she outclassed him. He was starting to think the couch wasn't far enough from her. He'd recuse himself and sleep in the yard.

She turned to him with a look of softness and wonder. "Did you write this?"

Oh crap, he thought. The manuscript from my jacket pocket! He'd thrown the jacket on the bed before he showered. Now it was folded over the back of a chair and the papers were in her hand. She must have found the manuscript when she moved the jacket.

"I did," he confessed.

The story wasn't meant for publication, or for any audience anywhere. Not even an audience of one. It was more of a personal exorcism, a semi-fictionalized account of everything that had gone wrong in his marriage to Leanne. It was a record of failure, missed opportunities and shameful selfishness, painful to write and unbearable to read. He had written it just to get it out, to acknowledge and face and then transcend the person he had once been. He was going to burn it after reading it three times, but so far, he hadn't managed to get through it once.

"These are the deepest, wisest words I've ever read," she said. He could see she meant it. He knew enough of her already to know she didn't lie.

"It's sad how many opportunities these two missed. If only they had talked to each other. Every time they reached a critical point, they got scared, they retreated into themselves instead of reaching out. And the worst of it is, they knew. They intuitively knew the other person was feeling the same thing, but neither wanted to risk reaching out, because they'd been so mean to each other in the past. Each was sure they were going to get burned. So, on they went in isolation and misery, each blaming the other."

Yup, thought McElwee. On they went, until they both broke.

"Your eyes are misting," she said. "You really felt this."

He sure did. And he was feeling something else now too. A growing admiration and respect for the woman who could summarize so eloquently the pages he'd composed with such agony. After his first and only attempt to read this work, he understood there were only two ways to react to it: with judgment or with compassion. If you judged the characters, you'd reject and condemn them. If you read compassionately, you accepted, commiserated, hurt with them; and that, he felt, was too much to ask of the average reader.

Both characters were awful, to each other and to themselves. Their relationship was a case study in emotional dysfunction. He knew from book group conversations, from reviews on Amazon and Goodreads, that many readers couldn't tolerate this kind of rawness. Their only defense against the difficult feelings a work like this aroused was to shut down all sympathy, to judge and condemn.

That had been his own reaction when he tried to read it. He hated himself and Leanne. They were failures, fearful and petty and stuck in a hell of their own making. They deserved the suffering they'd heaped on themselves.

He told himself he wouldn't burn the story until he had found compassion for them both. Maybe he'd been optimistic in thinking he'd reach that point by the third reading. He was still so pained by it all, he couldn't get past page six.

But Dorothy had responded instantly with compassion. She had already reached the place he felt he'd never get to, that place of acceptance and understanding.

How, he wondered. How do you get there? I mean, you, Dorothy. There's something in your nature, an open channel to kindness and decency. But in me, there's a blockage. I don't know what it is, and I don't know how to remove it.

His heart sank further. The backyard wouldn't be far enough from this woman he didn't deserve. He was going to have to sleep under a bridge.

"What kind of person sees these things?" Dorothy asked, waving the sheaf of papers. "All my life, this is how *I've* seen the world, and I've been entirely alone in what I see. Have you ever felt you're not of this world? That you're a stranger here, aware of things others can't see?"

"Oh yeah," McElwee said. And he didn't mean just now, in the Turnerverse, where he *was* a stranger. He'd felt that way his whole life. His friends seemed content to skim along the surface of the world, while he kept falling into the depths.

And if Dorothy felt alone—well, Turner wasn't known for sensitive or thoughtful characters. Or even interesting ones. Who could an intelligent person talk to in this world?

"Kiss me, Joey."

She kissed him before he could turn away. This was another man's lover. Sternjaw's, not McElwee's. Her heart was real and open and generous and not to be taken advantage of by some impostor who'd just wandered in by mistake.

Her eyes grew wide with wonder as she drew away. Had she read his mind? Was she horrified to realize the man she'd just kissed wasn't her Joey?

"Do you see that?" she asked.

"What?"

"Color. Those thin little stripes on your pajamas. They're in color!"

"And?"

"The world's been black and white for as long as I can remember, and now..." She traced the faint red and orange pinstripes on his pajamas. "Now there's color."

McElwee remembered thinking as a child that the world used to be black and white, because all the old photos and movies were black and white. Turner's writing certainly lacked color, and if Turner was trying to be true to the feel of the old detective films in his Joey Sternjaw series, maybe Turner had conceived for his characters a world of black and white. Morally, his stories were definitely black and white. The good guys were always right, and the bad guys were always horrible, and there was no in-between.

"How do you know what color is if you've never seen it?" he asked.

"Because I *have* seen it. My dreams are all in color. And every morning I wake to this flat world of greys. I tell you, Joey, I came from somewhere else, and the traces of that world are still in me, only no one can see them. I feel like the only parts of me that have ever been alive are the ones that fit into the constrained dimensions of this awful world. I know it's blasphemy, but I've always thought the god who created this place was an idiot. He's narrow-minded, short-sighted, and incapable of true depth. And he is a *he*. Not a man, but a boy. He likes guns and money and Veronica-sized boobs, and if he accidently put an honest heart in this world, he doesn't know it, and she just withers."

God, thought McElwee. What do I say to that?

"Come to bed," she said, pulling him down to the mattress.

She clicked off the lamp and whispered in his ear, "Joey! Understand me. Please?"

*Understand me*, he thought. That's *my* credo. That's what *I've* been looking for. Why else would I spend all that time alone, pouring my heart onto an empty page? Why? Because I haven't yet found the person who truly gets me and I haven't yet given up hope that they're out there. My novels are like the castaway's message in a bottle, floating vast, unfathomable seas, hoping to land in the hands of someone who cares.

She pulled his hand onto her smooth, flat belly. He felt her warm breath against his neck, and once again, he found himself doing the very thing he had vowed not to do.

# 16

He thought she was asleep. Her head rested on his shoulder, her breath deep and slow. He stroked her hair—the fine, thin strands—and felt the steady beat of her heart against his ribs.

Veronica was right. Sex is body and soul, mind and heart. You'll get no more out of it than you bring to it. Skin, hair, breath, anticipation, longing, satisfaction. Something in Dorothy inspired him, brought every part of him to life.

She was strangely tentative at first, especially given that she had initiated the act. During that brief period when she seemed to pull too far inward, too far away, as if she had to get over something internally, a flash of doubt told him she had figured out he wasn't her Joey, she sensed his imposture, and he thought they weren't going to hit it off. Then at last, whatever block she felt internally gave way and everything converged at once in the meeting of their bodies.

Communion, he thought, as he listened to her breath. Two spirits fully present, merging into one. Religions have ceremonies and rituals for this kind of communion because it feeds the spirit like nothing else.

He and Leanne used to screw. That was her word for it. They both had strong appetites, and they went at it with enthusiasm, impatience almost—like they were rushing to seize something before it could get away from them.

They were both in it for themselves, and for a deceptively long while, it worked out. The deception lay in their well-matched appetites, in the synchronicity of their desire, the way they'd trigger each other at the same time.

And trigger was the right word, McElwee thought. Other couples seemed to ramp up to desire, while he and Leanne exploded into it with little warning. They were both proud of the fact that their friends in less passionate relationships were jealous of their fire.

But passion, they learned, was an addiction. Like a drug, you needed more and more of it to stay afloat. You hollowed out in pursuit of it, neglecting the ordinary parts of life in search of the high. You pursued feeling without substance, and life kept getting emptier until one day you sat looking at each other wondering who you were and how you got here and why couldn't you just talk and enjoy each other's company like every other couple you knew.

The other person had been the source and provocateur of your emotions for so long that now that things were bad, it *had* to be their fault. You spent all your passion in fighting, love turned to hate, and the worst of it was you still couldn't break free. You kept thinking like the addict, thinking the initial bliss was still there to be had. You kept chasing it, kept fighting and hoping. And like the addict shooting his veins full of toxins, you filled your heart with poison, with hatred and resentment and recrimination.

Oh, God, thought McElwee, feeling the warmth of Dorothy's skin. I have to get away from her. I cannot poison this woman!

He nudged her gently off him and snuck to the bathroom. There, away from her, he could think more clearly, think how he could back out of this before he disappointed her. Or worse, corrupted her.

He shut the door softly, hoping not to wake her. Before he flipped the light switch, he smelled a familiar scent. The perfume of a neck he'd nuzzled hours earlier.

"She's so quiet," Veronica whispered as the room lit up.

McElwee saw her in the mirror, in a gown like Dorothy's, filled out with more generous proportions.

"How the hell did you get in here?" he asked.

"Through the window."

He had left it open after his shower to let the steam out of the room.

"You climbed that tree in your nightgown?" He was whispering, afraid of waking Dorothy.

Veronica shrugged. "I wanted to see what you were up to."

"This is private!" His voice a harsh, angry whisper.

"Obviously. But I hate it when authors skip over the bedroom scenes. I wanted to watch."

"You watched us? What the..." He was at a loss for words.

"She's so quiet, Joey!"

"Oh my God! This is... None of your damn business!"

"I used to hate it when guys were quiet during sex. I'd start thinking they weren't having fun, and then I'd get self-conscious. But there was this one guy—"

"Get out of here!"

"I'm talking!"

"Shut up and get out!"

"I'm trying to tell you something, Joe. You should listen. Seriously, half the problems in this world come from people not listening to each other."

"Say your piece and get out!"

"Well that's not the spirit I was hoping for. I don't know how you can listen to someone when you're angry and impatient."

"Jesus Christ!" McElwee put his head in his hands.

"That wasn't fucking, Joe."

"I know that."

"She's quiet because she's so intense. She's emotionally intense. Her life is on the inside, and you have to go in there and find her."

"I know."

"Good. And you found her. It's like drawing someone up from the depths. She's quiet and focused, almost like she's in prayer. She has to gather herself to let you in. And you can tell when she does. The way her breathing ramps up, you can hear she's losing control."

"I don't need your analysis. I was there."

"There's something almost holy about reaching that far into a person. About her letting you. When she finally did come, it was from the depths."

"Shut up, ok?"

"I came too," Veronica confessed.

"You what?"

"You didn't hear me, did you?"

McElwee shook his head in disbelief. "You what?"

"It was so erotic! That's what I was trying to tell you earlier. Screwing is fun, but the real magic is in the connection. What other act is so profound that it can summon whole new souls into being?"

"Oh, God," Joey whispered. "I hope she's not pregnant."

"Don't worry," Veronica said. "No consequences in the Turnerverse, remember? Listen, I want you to meet me in the diner tomorrow morning. I have some news for you."

"Fine. Now get out."

She blew him a playful kiss, and he watched with relief as she climbed out the window.

## 17

He vaguely remembered Dorothy leaving at five a.m. Her driver had come in the dark to pick her up. She didn't want to risk being seen.

At seven-thirty, he was at the sink, shaving, when a man fell over the sill of the window behind him and hit the floor with a thud.

McElwee turned to see Frump dusting himself off.

"Hey, Joey!"

"Frump?"

The detective straightened out his rumpled fedora—unsuccessfully, McElwee noted—and clapped it onto his head.

"Why didn't you just use the door?"

"The back door's been stuck since book two, Joey. The Marbury Case, remember? You really need to fix it. I'm getting too old to keep climbing through this window."

"Why didn't you use the front door?"

Frump looked puzzled. "I don't know. It never even occurred to me. But listen, I wanted to tell you I got distracted from the Astor case. Picked up a psychopath last night. He was hellbent on murdering a girl who'd stood him up."

"Was her name Suzette?"

"Yeah. How'd you know?"

"She's a waitress at the diner." The question was how did Veronica know? He made a note to ask her next time they met.

"He was going to stab her, Joey. He was stabbing her apartment door when we showed up. We sent the knife to ballistics to see if it's the same one used to kill Lady Astor."

McElwee wondered if it was worth pointing out that ballistics experts examined bullets, not knives. He let it drop.

Reading Turner was bad enough. He wasn't going to be his editor.

"I was wondering if you learned anything last night," Frump said.

"I think I did, but it's not applicable to the case. I heard you got a lead though. A serial number on a bill. Someone spent a twenty from Lady Astor's safe down on Murder Row."

"Yeah. It's disturbing, Joey. Very disturbing."

McElwee couldn't quite read his look. Was it an accusation? Was he disturbed because he'd traced the bill from the shop to Joey Sternjaw? The store owner would certainly remember him, the first customer of the day dropping a twenty on a six-cent purchase. Joey Sternjaw in his fine suit and hat...

"I need to follow up on another lead this morning."

"You want me to come with you?" McElwee asked.

"Actually, I'd rather you didn't."

That too was odd. Why make a point of excluding him?

"Is there something you're not telling me, Frump?"

"I'll tell you later," he said.

He tried to climb back out the window and got stuck.

"Say, Joey, could you give me a shove?"

McElwee pushed his foot into Frump's fat rump, and the old detective fell headfirst onto the ground. The ten-foot drop should have broken the big guy's neck, but... Turnerverse.

"You ok, Frump?"

"Fix that door," Frump called. He clapped his rumpled hat onto his balding head and padded off.

<h1 style="text-align:center">18</h1>

On his way out of the house, McElwee realized Veronica hadn't told him which diner to meet at. He decided it didn't matter. In the Turnerverse, if two characters were meant to be in the same scene, they'd both show up, no matter how improbable the circumstances.

To prove his point, he walked in the wrong direction, away from yesterday's lunch spot, toward Beverly Hills, where there should have been no diners, only homes.

Five minutes passed before he found the place. A diner that looked just like the other two. Veronica stood on the sidewalk out front, in a red satin dress, talking to the waitress from yesterday's lunch, the Suzette whose assailant Frump had arrested the night before.

"I wanted to thank you," the young woman said. "He came after us. Me, my sister, my friend. He was mad! Murderous! He almost stabbed his way through the apartment door. It took four policemen to subdue him. If it weren't for your warning, I'd be dead! Thank you! I'm going away now, to a place he'll never find me."

A greyhound bus pulled up beside the diner, despite there being no stop, and she boarded it with a wheeled suitcase. McElwee noted the anachronism. Those airplane carry-ons with the telescoping handles and black casters wouldn't exist for several decades.

Veronica read his mind. "I know. His books are full of them. There's only so much the editors can catch before the titles go to print."

Inside, she ordered a cup of coffee, a slice of key lime pie, a slice of apple pie, a slice of blackberry pie, and a bowl of vanilla ice cream.

"Won't you get sick eating that?" McElwee asked.

She shook her head. "Turnerverse. I won't get fat either. It's one of the few things I like about this place. You're just getting toast? That's it?"

"It's all I want right now. By the way, how did you know? About that waitress and the psychopath?"

Veronica rolled her eyes. "It was on *Dateline* three months ago. True crime. Turner watches that stuff and then he'll mash five or six real-life crimes into one over-the-top novel. Take the killer from one documentary, the victim from another, the setting from a third, change all the names, and voila! Another bestseller in his thriller line. He's a factory in search of raw material."

"But how did you know it was her?"

"The name tag and the rose tattoo on her wrist. And she looked like the actress who played the victim on the TV re-enactment. The girl—the real Suzette—was nineteen and innocent and sweet. Her family was devastated. I couldn't let that happen again. How's Dorothy?"

"Well enough, I suppose."

"Mmm. She got to you, didn't she?"

McElwee nodded.

"I can see it, Joe. The old Joe McElwee was worthy of her. And if you can't find him in there"—she tapped her fingers against his heart—"she will."

"I don't feel right taking another man's lover. She's in love with Joey Sternjaw. I'm an impostor pretending to be Joey."

"Joey Sternjaw is a Turner creation. *He's* the impostor, a stand-in for who Turner wishes he was. Tough enough to beat up Polski and handsome enough to bed Veronica Mayweather and Dorothy Astor. The fact that you and Dorothy found each other was just blind luck. People who have that kind of luck believe in destiny. People who don't—and that's most of us—understand the universe is arbitrary and indifferent to human suffering."

The waitress put three slices of pie on the table, followed by a plate of toast.

As Veronica dug in to the melting blackberries, the waitress told them she'd be back in a minute with the ice cream.

"What did you want to tell me?" McElwee asked.

"Oh yeah." Veronica wiped her mouth with a napkin. "Two things. One, I figured out where Dorothy came from."

"Where?"

"Remember I told you Turner works with ghost writers?"

"You said co-authors."

"There's one credited co-author on each book, but at least five or six contribute. He takes turns giving them credit."

"I wondered how he was able to crank out twelve titles a year."

"Now you know."

"You get this info from your friend in the publishing house?"

Veronica stuffed a forkful of key lime pie into her mouth. Her eyes went wide as she nodded yes to McElwee's question.

"Oh my God!" she exclaimed. She dug another forkful of key lime filling and put it in his mouth. "Turner made someone who could bake!"

McElwee was as impressed as she was.

"Where..." He sipped his coffee to clear his palate. "Where did Dorothy come from?"

"Mae Chang."

"What?"

"Mmm hmm."

"She's literary," McElwee said. "She's way out of Turner's league."

"Which is why she's always broke."

"You know she was once a student of mine?"

"I remember."

Every creative writing teacher in the country knew Mae Chang. No reader did. Her stories appeared in journals whose circulation was counted in the hundreds. McElwee and every other literate author he knew had learned from her. They had all lamented her unknown status, her having to scrape by teaching freshman comp at backwater colleges, her vividly described breakdowns. At the same time, they feared the day the public would discover her. She would expose them all as amateurs. Readers across the country would experience the same awakening he had when he'd read her first novel: "Oh my God, I've been reading crap. Everything I've read in the past four years has been garbage!"

"The publisher paid her a few thousand bucks," Veronica said. "Under the table, to write some 1940s LA society scenes for Turner. He couldn't pull it off on his own. So Mae Chang writes these dinners and parties, people all dressed up, with sparkling dialogue, social intrigue, sexual tension, repressed desires. All of it over Turner's head.

"She throws in this character Dorothy, this polished gem who's just layer upon layer of pearl, no matter how far you strip her down. And Turner's like, what the hell is this? She's not even pretty."

"She *is* pretty," McElwee insisted.

"Because Turner intervened. He thinks that because it's too much for him to have to look inside a character to find beauty, it's too much for his readers. Turner made Dorothy a blue-eyed blonde, and Mae Chang quit in tears. She ran back to her rural college with her tail between her legs to grade the papers of hungover eighteen-year-olds plagiarizing the Spark Notes summaries of *The Great Gatsby*. And Dorothy was left to languish in her own way. You know Turner doesn't know what to do with a character like her.

"But you, Joe! She's what you were getting close to before you gave in to Turner envy and sold out.

"What I said about Dorothy going inward last night, having to focus and draw herself together to let you in and really feel what you two were about—you know where that comes from, don't you? She was bred for poise. She's the picture of composed elegance, because that's what the world she came from wants from a woman. Not messy emotion. Not desire, or self-seeking, or growth and fulfilment.

"She's the embodiment of someone else's ideal. Her role was handed to her by her family and her society. Lady Astor's society. She didn't choose it, but she lives it fully. She's controlled all the time, demure. And when she finally does get a chance to connect, to reach down into real feeling with someone like you who gets it, she has to undo the constraints the world taught her to put on herself. That's no easy task, Joe. Believe me. That's why she starts out so quiet. She has to focus to connect. But the fact that she *can* get there, that she *can* do it, that's golden, Joe. I hope you appreciate her."

"I do," he said.

"Good. Now the other thing I wanted to talk to you about. The plot is starting to drag here. Mysteries aren't about romance. There's a crime to solve, and your dick got you sidetracked. You need to start investigating."

"Frump is doing that."

"Don't shirk, Joe. Dorothy gave you a number of clues and you haven't followed up on them."

"What clues?"

"I don't know. I was only there during the sex. What did you talk about before that?"

McElwee recalled his conversation with Dorothy at dinner the night before.

"She said her marriage is a sham."

"And?"

"Her husband, Walter, does things she doesn't like. And she said she had to be careful until the murderer was in custody, because as heirs to Lady Astor's fortune, the press would see her and Walter as having a motive to kill her."

"Well this is getting interesting," Veronica said. "Now that you're smitten, I'm sure it would just break your heart if sweet Dorothy was to blame for her granny's murder."

"She's not!" McElwee insisted.

He decided not to tell Veronica that Dorothy was in the house before and after the crime. That she was probably there during as well.

"A good detective doesn't let his emotions get in the way of his investigation," Veronica reminded him. "Has she officially hired you to look into this?"

"Not officially."

"I wonder why not?"

McElwee resented her twisting the knife. Veronica knew how to stoke his doubts and fears, and she seemed to enjoy doing it.

"The problem is," McElwee said as they exited the diner, "I don't know where she lives. It's not something you ask your longtime lover over dinner or in bed."

"Relax, Joe." Veronica stepped to the curb and hailed a cab.

McElwee thought the driver braked a little too hard, a little too eager to pick up the curvy woman in the tight red dress.

Veronica opened the door for him, then slid in herself.

"Where to?" asked the cabbie.

"The Astor mansion, Beverly Hills," she replied.

"Gotcha."

I should have known, thought McElwee. In the Turnerverse, everyone in LA would know where the famous Astors lived. Up in the hills, high above the petty material struggles of the bustling City of Angels.

The mansion turned out to be a white castle-like house behind a well-trimmed hedge. The iron gate guarding the cobblestone drive stood open. The grass of the broad front lawn was cut as short and smooth as a golf fairway. A gardener wearing a newsboy cap pushed a wheelbarrow beneath tall palms, collecting fallen fronds and occasional weeds.

The cab pulled up behind the two cars parked by the steps of the marble entrance. The brown Rolls, thought McElwee, must be Dorothy's car. She had mentioned she had a driver. The black Cadillac probably belonged to Walter.

"Three fifty-five," said the cabbie.

McElwee paid him and the two got out, Veronica hiking the tight dress down her thighs to as decent a length as it could reach.

The mansion's heavy double wood doors stood open. The maid sweeping the hall inside glanced up at them as they entered. She said nothing, but nodded her head toward the right rear of the house. McElwee wondered if there'd been so many cops going in and out since the murder that the staff had given up keeping track of visitors.

Surely, though, no one could mistake Veronica for a cop. Not in that dress. If the maid took a couple like him and Veronica in stride, perhaps there were other things going on in this mansion that an investigator should know about.

Veronica followed the sound of male voices to the rear study. There she found a man of forty or so with a pencil moustache sitting in an upholstered chair, smoking a cigarette in a long black tapered holder. His dark hair was short on one side, long on the other. Stringy bangs covered his right cheek and chin. His black silk pajama bottoms, printed with yellow and orange tropical birds, matched his smoking jacket.

A brown-skinned man of twenty-five or so, wearing a tight white tennis shirt and shorts, sat on the floor in front of him, rubbing the older man's bare feet. On the ottoman to the right of this pair, a sullen blond-haired boy of seventeen sat shirtless in blue swim trunks.

If this was Walter, if this was how he carried on in Dorothy's own home, McElwee understood her disgust.

"Hello, Joey." The words seemed to ooze from the man whose feet were being rubbed. "I see you've finally found yourself a real woman." He made a point of examining Veronica's figure, and of showing he wasn't interested.

"Hello, Walter." McElwee's flat tone betrayed his dislike for the man who had just disparaged his lover, insinuating that Dorothy, his own wife, wasn't a "real" woman.

"Dorothy's upstairs." Walter said. "I don't think she'd appreciate you bringing that roundheels here." He waved his cigarette toward Veronica to make sure she understood who he was talking about. The gesture stuck McElwee as feminine at first. But then he thought, no, women don't act like that. That was the limp-wristed wave of a flaming gay stereotype. Niall Turner always overdrew characters he didn't understand.

"Roundheels?" Veronica said angrily. "Who are you to judge, with your gunsel and your pool boy?"

It took McElwee a second to process the dialogue. A gunsel was a young boy kept by an older man for sexual favors. That would be the sullen blond-haired kid on the ottoman. Roundheels—a word he would have used himself if he ever got around to writing a midcentury crime novel—was a slut. As in, just give her a nudge and her round-heeled shoes would cause her to tip right over into bed.

"Manuel is a tennis pro, you grotesque caricature! You will respect him as such!" Walter flipped his head to the right in an attempt to clear the long bangs from the side of his face. When the hair fell back in place, he flipped his head again.

"Caricature?" Veronica huffed.

"You are kind of..." McElwee's hands traced an exaggerated hourglass figure in the air.

"Well I don't think the pot should be calling the kettle black," Veronica said.

"And what kind of pot am I?" Walter asked. "Hmm?" He took a long drag from his cigarette and let the smoke drift lazily from his nostrils. "Are you insinuating that I massage Manuel's strong muscles in a way other than to rejuvenate him for competition? Or that I take anything more than a fatherly interest in young Gunsel here? I'll have you know the boy couldn't swim when I found him out on Sunset Boulevard, and now he can go doggy... um..." He waved his cigarette in circles trying to think of the word. "Paddle for a very long time."

Veronica stared at him in silence. The anger clouding her face seemed to unnerve him. He flipped his head twice, trying to get the hair out of his face, then finally held it against his ear while he puffed nervously at his cigarette.

"What?" he asked. "Why are you looking at me like that?"

Veronica stepped to him, removed his cigarette from the holder, and stuck it back in his mouth.

"Why did you do that?" Walter asked.

"I've always thought Turner had issues with his sexuality," she said. "Bronco Howitzer is an over-the-top caricature of masculinity—"

"He is?" Walter asked, intrigued. "Can you introduce me?"

"—and you are an outdated gay stereotype."

Walter held his arm out and examined the silk sleeve of his smoking jacket. "But I just bought this last week. Surely it can't be out of fashion already."

"Turner can't write a gay man as an actual man," Veronica said. "He has to make him flaming, to be sure that no reader would ever confuse the character with the author himself. What's he so scared of?"

"I'm scared of spiders," Walter said, puffing nervously at his cigarette. "And steeply pitched roofs with loose tiles that slip out from under your feet."

"Stand up," Veronica said.

"I don't take orders from a woman."

"Stand up!" she barked, and Walter leapt to his feet. "Now let me see you walk."

Walter rolled his eyes. "I don't walk unless I have somewhere to go."

"Go get me some scissors."

"Alright," Walter said. "I have a lovely steel pair with inlaid pearl handles." He put his non-cigarette hand on his hip and walked toward a polished wood side table with short steps and swinging hips.

"Don't mince!" Veronica commanded.

"But it's my signature walk! Who would I be if I walked like, like..." Again, he waved his cigarette in a flamboyant gesture of contempt, this time toward McElwee. "Like Joey Sternjaw over here? I'd just be ordinary."

"You'd be an actual person," Veronica said. "Why don't you try it?"

"Alright. Look how boring I am now!" He walked to the table with normal steps, and then returned to Veronica and placed the scissors in her hand.

"That actually felt more natural," he confessed.

"Because your bones and muscles were made to walk that way. Come here."

"What are you going to do?"

"Cut those bangs," Veronica said. "You're forty years ahead of your time. That hairdo is from a nineteen-eighties band called A Flock of Seagulls."

Walter stepped forward and puffed his cigarette while she cut his bangs. At one point, she even took the cigarette from his lips, took a drag, and then put it back.

"There," she said. "Now you can see out of both eyes."

"But what excuse will I have for tossing my head to the side?"

"There's no excuse for that. Just stop it."

Walter returned to his chair looking uncertain and forlorn, as if he'd just been deprived of his identity. He stubbed out his cigarette in the ashtray beside the chair and lit another.

"Why did Dorothy marry you?" McElwee asked. "The way you're drawn, anyone could see you're not interested in women."

"She had to," Walter said. "Lady Astor had put too much of the family fortune into a failing oil company. The way it looked at the time, they'd be out on the street in six months. My family wanted to get rid of me, for obvious reasons. They were delighted to hear I was marrying. Dorothy didn't like being pushed into it, but since when does she have a say in anything? She cried our entire wedding night. Manuel and I could hear her outside the closet door.

"But, you see, my share of my family's fortune was enough to prop up the Astor's failing oil company. They bought fields in Texas and Oklahoma and were rolling in money again by the end of the year. That was when the old bag started to show her true colors."

"What old bag?" McElwee asked.

"Lady Astor. She wanted me gone. Wanted to marry her granddaughter off to a man who'd give her an heir."

"Did you and Dorothy ever, uh..." McElwee wasn't sure how to finish the sentence.

"Get busy?" Walter asked. "Please! What's that little willow got that I would want?"

"I don't get it," McElwee said. "Why wouldn't she have annulled the marriage?"

"Annul? What's that?" asked Walter.

Veronica rolled her eyes. "Another Turner plot hole," she explained. "Any normal person would have annulled a sham marriage that left them trapped and miserable, especially when they have strong grounds. Non-consummation is ground one for annulment. This is the kind of thing that makes Turner's protagonists so hard to root for. They're supposed to be intelligent and sensible, but the whole reason they're in trouble in the first place is for something stupid and senseless, some decision that's out of character. We root for imperfect protagonists when their troubles come from genuine character traits, from their relatable imperfections, not when their problems come from being stupid and ignoring common sense. Or not knowing basic commonsense things, like that an unconsummated marriage can be annulled."

"Wait a minute," Walter said. "Is Dorothy the protagonist?"

"We don't know yet," McElwee said. "She could be the murderer."

"But... I thought I was the protagonist." Walter sounded crestfallen.

"We all are," Veronica offered. "Of our own lives anyway."

"Who is this Turner fellow?" Walter asked. "Who put hair in my eyes and made me mince?"

"An author," Veronica said.

"He sounds awful," Walter said. "I think I hate him. Manuel? Gunsel? What do you think?"

"I don't like being a kept boy," said Gunsel.

"He makes me eat tacos and refried beans," said Manuel. "I'm Spanish, not Mexican."

"Well I think we should all go on strike," said Walter.

"There's no time for that," McElwee said. "We have a murder to solve. Where were you on the night Lady Astor was killed?"

"In the garden shed, with Manuel."

"Did you hear anything?"

"Nothing at all, until Detective Frump pulled up in his police car."

"Did you come inside? Look at the scene?"

"I didn't have the heart. I can't stand the sight of blood, so I went upstairs."

"Who else was in the house that night?" asked McElwee.

"Just Dorothy."

"No servants?"

"None," said Walter. "The maid leaves at six. The butler had the day off. And I sent the gardener home so Manuel and I could have the shed to ourselves."

"What about visitors? Did anyone come to the house that day?"

"Just Frump. He was here earlier in the evening."

"Doing what?" asked McElwee.

"Having tea with the old bag, I suppose."

"With Lady Astor? Why would they have tea?"

"She liked his stories."

"Frump?" McElwee was puzzled. "He barely talks. Gives you the facts, and that's all. What kind of stories would he have to tell?"

Walter shrugged. "I don't know."

"Where's Dorothy?"

"Upstairs. In her room."

McElwee turned to Veronica. "You'd better stay here. You're already on her shit list for showing up at my house and leaving that note."

"I'm on my own shit list," she said, "for being built like Jessica Rabbit. Go talk to her."

<h1 style="text-align:center">20</h1>

McElwee walked halfway up the red carpeted stairway before he realized why it felt so familiar. Turner, who watched films but didn't read, had copied it from Twelve Oaks, the plantation house in *Gone with the Wind*.

While Joey Sternjaw would know which room belonged to his lover, Dorothy, Joe McElwee had to guess. He opened the first door on the left to find a heart-shaped bed with a pink velvet cover and furry white pillows. Not at all what he would have expected from the refined Dorothy Astor. Then he saw the ashtray on the nightstand. This was Walter's bedroom, part of the stereotype Turner had created in place of a character.

McElwee recalled an episode of the Mystery and Thriller podcast he'd heard a few months ago while boiling ramen noodles in his basement kitchenette. The host was interviewing Niall Turner about his shift from writing contemporary novels to historical crime fiction.

Turner said part of the reason for his move back into the past was that the current reality of constant digital surveillance made mystery nearly impossible. Everyone was being tracked all the time. If a detective wanted to know whether a suspect was near the scene of a crime when it occurred, he could go online and buy the suspect's cell phone location history.

"Seriously," Turner said. "There are websites that sell that stuff. All you have to do is check the box that says 'I am not law enforcement,' because the fourth amendment prohibits selling location data to cops, but not to private citizens. Then you type in your credit card number and you have your answer."

McElwee had spent a good bit of time writing around issues like that in *Extraordinary Joe*. The bad guys all used burner phones, and the main character had to accidentally drop his Android into a river to avoid being tracked by assassins. McElwee was proud of that bit of plotting. What initially looked like an unfortunate accident—the protagonist losing his phone over the side of a bridge—turned out to be a blessing in disguise.

"And then there are surveillance cameras," Turner told the interviewer. "They're everywhere, and they're hooked into facial recognition systems. If you have access to the right databases, you can practically say, Show me everywhere suspect X appeared on these dates, and you can catch them in the act.

"Add in social media, and you know who all your suspect's friends are. You know where he hangs out, and when, and who he's with. How can there be any mystery in a world like that?"

McElwee had run into the same problems. In *Extraordinary Joe*, he had to give his villains hacking skills to shut down the digital systems that would otherwise give them away. The whole mystery-thriller genre, he felt, had lost some of its soul in this endlessly interconnected world.

"Before the internet," Turner told his interviewer, "a detective had to put in good, old-fashioned legwork to catch a criminal. I wanted to go back to that with Joey Sternjaw. Back to that golden age when a cop was a cop and a man was a man."

That last comment had hit a nerve. When was a man ever *not* a man, McElwee wondered? He had had an inkling, when he heard those words, that Turner wanted to move his novels back in time not just to escape modern technology, but also to escape changing social roles he couldn't seem to grasp or accurately portray in his fiction.

The world was easier to draw when society's lines were clearer and harder to cross. In 1948, men were the heroes who had just returned from the war to sweep women off their feet. In reality, that meant pushing them out of well-paying jobs, back into the home to raise children.

Men were the action figures in the world, the agents of good and evil, forgers of their own destinies. Women came along for the ride, adornments to the hero's bed, subjects of crime scene photos, evidence of a villain's handiwork, occupants of graves dug too soon.

McElwee reflected with a tinge of regret that his own recent work had fallen into this tradition. Though set in the iPhone age, *Extraordinary Joe* was of the same mold as a Joey Sternjaw stick-it-to-the-bad-guy caper.

He tried to console himself with the reassurance that he had never written a two-dimensional stereotype as flat and false as Walter. But what had stopped him? Walter would be unacceptable to a twenty-first-century audience. That was all. He would not have slipped past the developmental editor.

In the crime fiction of the '30s and '40s, however, he was a familiar trope. In that era of rigid gender roles, a writer could count on almost universal agreement from his audience that the homosexual was a degenerate. Dashiell Hammett had used the prejudice to great effect in *The Maltese Falcon*, in the character of the oozing Joel Cairo. Come to think of it, that was where the word "gunsel" had entered the crime fiction lexicon.

Cairo's sexuality marked him as a villain as clearly as Polski's snarl marked him as a thug. Readers wanted him to be the bad guy. They just had to stick around till the end to see him get his punishment.

McElwee closed the door on the bedroom with the garish pink spread and made a mental note. In the Turnerverse, where the badness of the bad guys was always overdrawn, Walter would be a likely culprit. The tone-deaf Turner expected the reader to root against this caricature, the man who was not a man, who picked up gunsels on Sunset Boulevard, badmouthed his dead grandmother-in-law, and forced the lovely Dorothy to suffer a barren, loveless marriage.

<h1 style="text-align:center">21</h1>

The next door opened to a room as richly furnished as the spirit of the woman who inhabited it. Dorothy stood at the window in a blue silk robe lined with golden dragons, taking in the sweeping southern view of Los Angeles. To the west, the Pacific glistened in the late morning sun.

"Hello, Joey."

She hadn't turned. He had opened the door without a sound, yet she knew he was there.

"I always know it's you," she said, turning at last to face him. "You know, I never realized those flowers in the yard were magenta. Or that the trees that line these dry yellow hills were such a deep shade of green. The ocean, until yesterday, was gray. The same as this robe. I think we need to be reminded now and then that we're alive, or else the color drains from the world and our favorite foods lose their flavor. Isn't that what they call depression, Joey?"

She walked toward him now and they met in the middle of the room. "Isn't that the spirit wilting in isolation," she said, "like wisps of dying grass deprived of sun?"

Her kiss sent a jolt of lightning through his heart.

She took his hand and said, "Gram couldn't make up her mind if I should live in a library or a museum."

He noted the black lacquered furniture inlaid with gold, the ancient Chinese vases on the shelves, the small terra-cotta soldiers, replicas from the Forbidden City.

"She went through a phase," Dorothy said, "collecting all she could from the Orient."

It wasn't Gram, thought McElwee. Mae Chang made you. He could see it now in the dark roots of her hair, beneath the blonde dye. Turner had lightened her hair and cast her eyes to a bright sky blue, but he hadn't bothered to change the furnishings, her robe, or the delicate watercolors of fog-shrouded Asian mountains that lined the walls. Turner farmed out the grunt work of worldbuilding to ghost writers, and apparently no significant scene from the Sternjaw series had yet unfolded in this room, or Turner's laborers would have Westernized the decor to suit its blonde inhabitant.

"One annoying thing about this place," Dorothy said, "is— Well, you know how much I love to read. But the books here..." She motioned toward the shelves. "Take a look."

The wall opposite the window was lined with expensive hardcovers with ridged spines. McElwee crossed the room to examine the volumes. Squinting at the spines, he said, "They have no titles. How do you know what's in them?"

"You open them," Dorothy said, returning to the window.

He pulled a book from the shelf, a dark blue volume with gilded pages, opened it and flipped through.

"It's empty," he said, surprised.

"They all are," said Dorothy.

He pulled another from the shelf, bound in beautiful brown leather that seemed to promise rich rewards inside. He fanned through the empty snow-white pages.

"God, that's sad," he said.

"Is it?" she asked.

"Don't you think?"

Dorothy shrugged. "If you choose to see it that way."

"What other way is there?"

"They're waiting to be written. Like souls waiting to born."

She crossed from the window and stood beside him.

"But I do get tired of waiting. I burn for a good story, something to light my mind and heart. I even read *your* story again, sad as it was. At least those two were alive. Suffering tells you that. That you're alive. The fire those two descended into wasn't pleasant, but I think it woke them up. I think it told them, if you can feel pain this deeply, you can feel joy as well. Go out now and find it! At least, that's where I like to imagine the story going. It seems incomplete. Is there going to be a second part?"

"I hope so," McElwee said.

"I'll tell you something, Joe." She lowered her voice. "The fiery sex those two had is something I've never felt in real life. But the fact that I could feel it in the words, I think it's something I'm capable of. I want to go there sometime. Not in the destructive way they did. I think if you stand on solid ground with your partner, you can delve into that fire without being consumed by it."

She sniffed at his lapel and her eyes narrowed.

"What?" he asked.

"You've been with that woman again. I know her perfume."

"We had breakfast together."

"Why?"

"Talking about the case."

"Oh? She's your assistant now?"

"She's helping out. But I didn't touch her. I'll never touch her again, I promise."

"So you *have* touched her before?"

McElwee nodded.

She turned away from him and walked back to the window. "To be honest, I'd have trusted you less if you hadn't. Only a man like Walter could resist a woman like her, and the last thing I want in a lover is another Walter. Manuel seems pleased with him, though, so I suppose he's good for something."

"Listen," said McElwee. "I wanted to ask you about the night of the murder."

"What about it? I already told you."

"Tell me again."

She explained to him that there had been no supper that evening. The cook had left after lunch.

"The cook?" McElwee asked. Walter had mentioned a maid, a butler, and a gardener, but no cook.

"The cook, Joey! The one who made the food I brought to your house last night. You don't think Gram and I cook our own meals in a place like this?"

"No, I suppose not."

McElwee sat on the arm of a chair and watched her as she leaned against the windowsill and pulled her hair back. She told him she had eaten leftovers from the kitchen that evening. She assumed Gram had done the same.

"Where was Walter?" McElwee asked. He wanted to see if her story squared with her husband's.

"In the shed with Manuel."

"What about the gunsel?"

"I gave him fifty dollars and had my driver take him to a Chinese restaurant by the train station."

"Isn't fifty a lot for Chinese food?"

"I'm trying to get him to run back home, but he won't. If I weren't married to Walter, I'd have called the police on him."

"That would be a good way to get rid of a bad husband."

"Gram forbade it. She hated scandal, and in her world, scandal isn't *doing* something wrong, it's *getting caught* doing something wrong. Walter had the perfect setup. I was his beard and Gram kept the moat around the castle."

"Ok. So the staff is gone, Gunsel is gone, and Walter and Manny are in the shed. That leaves you and Gram."

"And Frump. Gram had him to tea."

"I just can't picture Frump drinking tea."

"Gram was teaching him," Dorothy said. "And he was teaching her about broads and wise guys, skid row, the clink, and Palookaville. It was like a cultural exchange. Gram always liked the thrill of slumming, but she hated actually going to the slum because she couldn't wear her diamonds."

"What time did Frump leave?"

"Around seven."

"And what time did you find your grandmother in the study?"

"Ten-thirty. She was lying in a pool of blood. I couldn't go in. The sight was so shocking I turned and ran. I called the operator from the hallway phone. They sent Frump because, well... The rich like to keep their scandals out of the news. If we have to go to the police, we deal with our contacts in the department."

"You didn't hear anything? No sounds of struggle?"

"No. I was here in my room, daydreaming. Staring at the shelves, projecting fantasies onto those blank pages. I swear, I'd live almost any other life than this one. Material wealth does not make up for spiritual poverty."

"But your Gram was stabbed and you didn't hear?"

Dorothy shook her head. "The walls are thick, and the bath was running. I kept the door open to make sure the tub didn't overflow."

McElwee looked at the bathroom door to his right. If Dorothy had been standing at the window where she stood now, she could have kept an eye on both the running bath and the inscrutable wall of unwritten literature.

"How long did it take Frump to get here?"

"After I called?" she asked. "Two minutes."

"Seems kind of fast."

"I guess I hadn't thought about that."

"Was anyone else in the house between the time the staff cleared out and when you found your Gram?"

"Just the movers."

"What movers?" And why had Walter not mentioned them? Could he and Manuel have missed them while they were in the shed?

"Boss Harley's piano movers. The concert grand in the drawing room had gotten out of tune, so Gram had it swapped out for a new one."

"What? Why didn't she just have it tuned?"

"Gram did lots of peculiar things."

"No, Dorothy. Niall Turner needed an excuse to get Boss Harley's thugs into the house, so he came up with this cockamamie idea of swapping out the pianos, then justified it by saying old Gram Astor was eccentric."

"Well, she was."

"I'm sure she was. But the real world doesn't work that way. When a piano's out of tune, you tune it. You don't replace it.

This is why I can't stand Turner. I just don't get why people put up with his nonsense."

"Who's Turner?"

"Never mind. What did these movers look like?"

"There were four of them, all big and strong."

McElwee tried to remember the faces of the four thugs who had spilled out of the Packard in front of the diner on Murder Row yesterday. The only one he could recall clearly was Polski.

"Was one of these movers tall? Like six foot six, thinning hair, with a red pock-marked face?"

"Yes. Polski."

"He told you his name?"

"It was written in black marker on the band of his underpants. I saw it under his coin slot when he bent down."

"Coin slot?"

"His plumber's smile. You know, the crack some people show when they bend over without a belt."

"Got it. Thanks for the visual. How long were they here?"

"An hour. They left around eight-thirty."

The phone rang as McElwee plotted out his next move. First, he'd talk to Gunsel, ask him where he'd been that night and what time he had returned.

Then he'd pay a visit to Boss Harley's hideout. Or headquarters, whatever it was. He wanted to know more about this piano, and whether Polski and his crew had used the piano move as a cover to case the house.

"No," said Dorothy into the receiver. "No, I don't think I could take it. Thank you for the invitation, but I'll listen on the radio from here. It's all so overwhelming."

When she hung up, McElwee asked who had called.

"Frump. He says he's cracked the case."

"Already?"

"He's holding a press conference in thirty minutes at the police station to announce an arrest. He asked if I wanted to come. I don't."

"Crap." McElwee picked up his hat from the chair.

"Where are you going?" Dorothy asked.

"To the police station."

# 22

Returning to the study downstairs, McElwee was surprised by Walter's transformation. Though he still wore the silk smoking jacket and pajama bottoms, Veronica had cleaned up his hair and he now spoke like a person audiences would listen to instead of mock. He was showing Veronica clippings from the society pages of the *LA Daily*.

There was Dorothy on Walter's arm at a charity ball. There was Dorothy beside Lady Astor at the opening of the new art museum. There was Dorothy surrounded by children at the orphanage her family's riches had paid for. In each photo, she was an accessory to a story about someone else.

"Veronica," McElwee said softly.

She looked up from the clippings, startled. "I didn't hear you come in."

"We have to go to the police station. Frump is making an announcement." To Walter, he added, "You have a phone? So I can call a cab?"

"Take the Rolls," Walter said. "The driver needs to earn his keep."

Five minutes later, they were on their way.

"Oh, I love this," Veronica said, stroking the soft leather of back seat. "Reading about the interior of a Rolls is one thing. Being in one is something else. It's so smooth and quiet, like you're gliding through the world in your own luxurious bubble."

McElwee cut her off with a practical question. "Hey, what was the name of that story Mae Chang wrote? About the Chinese-American girl who goes to beach week with all the white kids the summer she graduates high school?"

"Excursion?"

"That's it."

"That's a good one," Veronica said.

"It is. I'm starting to see traces of the author in Dorothy's character. Remember, when the girl in 'Excursion' is packing for the trip, she's thinking about all the roles she has to play at home. Daughter, sister, aspiring student. A potential source of pride or shame to her parents, depending on how her life pans out. And then she'll be a wife and a mother, and she starts to feel smothered by it all.

"Her existence is just flitting from role to role, and none of them are broad enough to contain her true self. She doesn't know what her 'true self' even is. All she knows is she feels constrained."

"You see that in Dorothy?" Veronica asked.

"Yes. I mean, she's trapped in that house, that society, that marriage."

"She's not trapped, Joe. She has you. It's part of her deal with Walter."

"Yeah, well, I don't think she's where she wants to be. And looking at all those photos of her… What's her role? Her role is to look good, to be the pretty wife to Walter in front of the cameras, the dutiful granddaughter of the rich old dowager, the nurturing supporter of lowly orphans.

"You remember, in the story, how much Chang's character is looking forward to a week away from all that? She thinks the white kids have this absolute freedom. And at the beach, they drink and skinny dip and have long hangover brunches on the boardwalk. The girls make out with boys in the hot tub and watch hours of Netflix and shop for clothing they'll never wear back home.

"In the last two days of the trip, she starts to feel this overwhelming emptiness. She feels that she and all the kids around her are just these hollow sacks of desire in constant pursuit of fulfillment. They flit from the store to the restaurant to the hot tub to the television, cycling through the desires to own, to consume, to be pleased and entertained.

"And then there's that scene on the last night, when she's locked in her room listening to couples in the rooms on both sides of her, kids who barely know each other, having drunken sex. The rest of the crew is in the hot tub, drinking and laughing and telling loud, dumb stories, and she just wants to leave. She wants to disappear, but there's no place to go.

"So she picks up a book, a paperback of Shakespeare's sonnets, and she tries to lose herself in that. She reads through a dozen poems, and she starts to notice the structure. Three quatrains, rhyming every other line, followed by a couplet. Every poem follows the same pattern. And within the lines, there's an even simpler structure: iambic pentameter. Exactly ten syllables, with every other syllable accented.

"Why would Shakespeare, she wonders, an artist who, by definition, seeks creative expression—why would he impose such a strict format on his work? Wouldn't he be freer to express himself if there were no rules?

"And then she has the big a-ha moment. The fact that he has to stick to this format *forces* him to be creative. He can't just throw together the first words that come to mind. He has to choose them carefully to make sure they don't violate the rhythm and the rhyme. And so the words he chooses are *not* the expected ones that come up in everyday conversation. They're surprising words, and they bring a richness and a depth you don't see in free-form conversation.

"She goes back home with this new acceptance. Yes, the roles she's expected to adhere to may be constraining, but they impose a kind of discipline, and if you master that discipline, you can actually develop a pretty rich existence within their bounds. At the same time, she sees the freedom she once envied in the white kids as a kind of bondage. They're all just waiting for the next sensation to remind them they're alive.

"Dorothy is totally Mae Chang's character. She lives in the role-bound world of old money and high society. She's done everything expected of her. She let that world mold her into its ideal, but she didn't let it erase her.

"You know, that posture of hers, her poise and eloquence, the clarity of her diction—all those are marks of discipline. She's mastered herself, which is something few people ever do. And she's still alive in there." He tapped his heart to indicate which 'there' he meant. "That's what makes her so attractive."

"You sound smitten, Joe."

"I am. She has imagination. I like that in a person. Imagination is the life of the soul turned inward. The Turnerverse wasn't built to fulfill a thinking, feeling woman, so she makes a richer world in her mind and dwells in that. I've always thought people like her make the best readers. The writer's canvas is the reader's mind, and even a Tolstoy or a Shakespeare can't do much with a dullard."

"No," said Veronica, "but Turner can. He delivers the sensations those empty kids at the beach keep waiting for. You have to give him credit for that. And now you're going after his audience instead of minds like hers. You should think about that, Joe. Is this the police station?"

It was.

The Rolls came to a halt and they got out.

# 23

The great marble hall of the station was packed. Even though the cops had set up fans along the walls, the air was hot and thick with the sweat of reporters, photographers, city clerks, and curious citizens who had wandered in from the streets.

The chatter of the crowd and the drone of the fans echoed from the vaulted ceilings and marble walls. McElwee and Veronica pushed their way to the front of the crowd, just as Detective Frump was stepping up to the podium. McElwee noted that Frump was sweating and looked even more haggard than usual.

Frump tapped the chrome microphone and said, "Alright, everyone, quiet down. We're here for an announcement about the Astor case, and I'm going to give it to you."

He pulled a handkerchief from his pocket, wiped his brow, and then continued.

"We picked up our first clue yesterday. A bill stolen from the safe of Lady Astor was used to make a purchase near Murder Row."

The crowd gasped.

"We were able to match the serial number to a list the victim had written in her own hand. The merchant described the man who had given him the bill."

Now McElwee began to sweat. He wanted to take off his jacket. Knowing that he may have been the one who had spent that bill, he felt guilty and cornered. Had Frump lured him to his own arrest? McElwee turned and surveyed the uniformed officers lined up along the walls. They weren't looking at him. Their eyes were glued to Frump at the podium. They were awaiting his word, McElwee thought. Frump just had to point him out and they'd pounce.

He turned to Veronica and whispered, "Let's get out of here."

"Shhh! I want to know who did it!"

"The next clue," Frump said, "was this." He pulled a diamond necklace from his pocket, and again the crowd gasped.

McElwee tried to remember if that necklace was in the pile of loot he'd awakened to the day before. He couldn't tell. One diamond necklace looked like another to him. It was actually a problem, according to his editor, who told him, "Look, Joe, if you're going write for the mass market, at least get your name brands straight. I don't need fancy characters or plots that make sense, but I do need product placements. This bracelet you wrote onto your victim's wrist is *not* a Cartier. They don't do emeralds and pearls with silver. No one does."

The editor slammed a pile of magazines onto the desk and said, "I want you to study all these back covers, then describe what you see. Put *that* on your victim's wrist if you want to pick up an extra ten grand in sponsorship."

Part of him had balked at the indignity of shilling for a company that pulled diamonds from mines in third world countries and assembled them into products he would never have been able to afford as a literary writer. Another part of him tabulated the outstanding bills: rent, utilities, insurance, car repair. In the end, he decided he didn't care what was on his victim's wrist when she was murdered. If someone else cared enough to lay ten thousand dollars on the line for a cheesy product placement, well, who was he to stand in the way of their foolishness?

"And the clincher," Frump continued.

He pulled a ring from his right coat pocket in a dramatic gesture. That one McElwee did recognize. It had stood out from the rest of the jewels, glinting red beside a pile of twenties. An enormous square ruby mounted on a gold band, utterly without taste. While the stone was undoubtedly worth a fortune, its exaggerated size made it look more like a hooker's costume jewelry than something you'd find on the hand of an elderly socialite. Putting a ring like that in the safe of Lady Astor was an unmistakable Turnerism.

"Who passed the stolen twenty on Murder Row?" Frump asked in a dramatic rhetorical flurry.

Maybe it was me, McElwee thought. But maybe it was someone else.

McElwee thought back to the previous morning. He had returned to the apartment and found it empty. Whoever had been there, whoever had scooped up the cash and jewels, could have spent that twenty on Murder Row.

Could it have been Frump? Was it he who cleaned the place out? No. McElwee had walked directly from the diner to The Loaded Arms. Frump had been out of his sight only ten minutes. He wouldn't have had time to gather all the loot, clean up the blood, fix the broken mirror, and swipe the cat.

But in a Turner novel? Who knows, McElwee thought. He's committed more egregious violations of common sense.

"So who had possession of this necklace and this ring?" Frump asked. "Who's our suspect?"

He had the crowd on the tips of their toes. Who knew the guy was such a showman? Maybe this was the storytelling ability Walter had mentioned, the reason Lady Astor had invited Frump to tea.

"Well," Frump said, "it was someone we know was in the house the evening of the murder."

Polski? Could it have been him, McElwee wondered.

"The perpetrator," Frump said ominously. "The robber... the murderer..."

As the photographers raised their cameras to capture the big reveal, Frump collapsed into tears and blurted, "Was me! I did it!"

Two uniformed officers standing along the wall behind him leapt forward and cuffed him as the crowd broke into a roar of confusion.

"Oh my God!" Veronica said in disgust. "Turner already used that trick. The detective being the perpetrator. There's a reason mystery writers have a rule against the investigator committing the crime. It's unsatisfying. The reader feels hoodwinked. It's a cheap trick."

"It's a false ending," McElwee said.

"It certainly rings false."

"No, I mean false like the story isn't actually over yet. Everyone's supposed to think Frump did it, including Frump, so the heat is off the real perpetrator. As long as the public thinks the case is wrapped, the real perp can walk free. Maybe that's what they're counting on. He'll be emboldened, attempt another crime, only he'll slip up this time and they'll catch him. Come on, let's get out of here."

On the steps outside, they breathed fresh air. McElwee was mulling over his next move when a short, stocky woman buried her head in his chest and began to wail.

"I always knew he'd come to no good," she bawled.

"Who?" asked McElwee.

"Frump!"

The woman backed off and lifted her apron to wipe her eyes. She was dowdy, with a bun of gray hair, and once her hands were free of the apron, she wrung them dramatically in worry.

Veronica leaned in and whispered, "Edna Frump. The detective's wife. All she does is iron and wring her hands. This is the first time Turner's ever gotten her out of the house."

"I'm going back home to Mother," she declared. "Back to Buffalo and the long, cold winters!"

She picked up two gray suitcases that hadn't been there a minute ago, descended the stairs, and boarded a bus marked "Buffalo."

"Where the hell did that come from?" McElwee asked.

"Turner's very efficient at shunting characters offstage when he's done with them. What are you thinking? Because at this point, I'm lost. I mean, I can follow a book that makes sense. But this..."

"We have to get into the jail and talk to Frump."

"Why?"

"What other leads do we have?"

<h1 style="text-align:center">24</h1>

"No way I'm lettin' youse guys in," said the guard. He was a heavyset man of forty or so whose eyes kept wandering to Veronica's bust.

"Why can't I go in?" McElwee asked.

"You wore out your welcome wit dis department da day you nailed da police chief."

McElwee looked at Veronica, wondering if "nailed" meant "busted" or "had sex with." Veronica shrugged.

"Sure he was crooked," the guard continued. "But a cop's a cop. We don't turn on our own. Now beat it!"

"But that's just it," McElwee said. "I think Frump is innocent. If we talk to him, we might be able to help him out of this jam."

"You think I'm gonna help you get a crook out of jail?" The guard's eyes narrowed as he eyed McElwee with suspicion.

"You just said cops shouldn't turn on their own."

"Stop confusin' me or I'll lock up the both a ya's."

"Could you lock us in the same cell as Frump?" Veronica asked.

"No broads in the slammer," said the guard, trying his best to pry his eyes from the curves of her tight red dress. "Now get outta here."

"Is there nothing we can do to convince you?"

"Nuttin'."

Veronica leaned in and whispered, "You seem like a man of taste and good sense."

His eyes were glued to her cleavage.

"Wouldn't you like to help a fellow cop get out of jail?" She ran her finger playfully under his chin, leaning forward to give him a good long look.

"Ok," said the wide-eyed guard, licking his lips and shifting his weight from foot to foot. "Just dis once. But I don't want no funny stuff from either one a ya's."

## 25

Frump sat on his cot against the wall, hat on head, collar open, tie loosened, sipping a bottle of whiskey, his rumpled suit soaked with sweat.

"This is it, Joey. Tomorrow, I get the chair."

"You haven't even been arraigned yet."

"They're gonna fry me."

"They have to try you first," McElwee said, "and I think we can get you out of here before it comes to that. How did you get that bottle of whiskey?"

"The guard gave it to me. How's Edna?"

"She went home to Buffalo."

"Is that where she's from?" Frump mused.

"Do you honestly think you did this, Frump?"

"I'm a detective, Joey. I gotta follow the evidence, even if it points to me."

"Do you remember killing Lady Astor?"

Frump shook his head.

"Where did the bill come from? The one that was spent on Murder Row?"

"A shopkeeper. He said a guy came in as soon as he opened the morning after the murder. Bought a notebook and a pencil. Put down a twenty on a six-cent purchase."

McElwee's heart skipped a beat. "Wait, did he describe this guy?"

"Yeah. Said he wore a suit and hat, looked like a detective. I tell you, Joey, that set off the alarm bells."

In Turner's readers, McElwee thought. Or it should have anyway. He wondered if Turner's editors had gone slack once they realized how much nonsense his audience would put up with.

"Only one guy fits that bill." Frump pointed his thumb at his own chest and frowned. "I was lucky to get out of there without crapping myself. That was yesterday. This morning, I woke up on a park bench with a necklace and a ring in my pocket."

"No you didn't. You were in my bathroom this morning, remember? You came in while I was shaving."

"I wanted to see you one last time before they fried me. You've been a good pal, Joey. A real good pal."

The guard returned and stood outside the open cell door. "Hey Sternjaw," he said. "You got a call."

"Here?"

The guard pointed down the hallway.

"Who the hell knows I'm here?"

The guard pointed again. "Payphone. Far wall, next to the desk."

As McElwee passed, the guard gave Veronica a hopeful smile. He made a gesture of leaning forward, pulling down his shirt. Veronica shook her head. Show's over. No more for today. He frowned in disappointment and followed McElwee to the phone.

McElwee lifted the earpiece and almost answered with his real name. Catching himself at the last second, he said into the mouthpiece, "Joey Sternjaw, who's calling?"

The voice on the other end of the line chilled his soul.

"Rrrrr-now?"

The scoundrel who had his Tabitha laughed maniacally and hung up.

## 26

On their way out of the jail, McElwee explained that Frump had been framed.

"I haven't told you this," he confided. "I haven't told anyone, because I was afraid to go to the chair myself."

He paused for a moment, noting he was starting to talk like a Turner character.

"Don't fight it," Veronica said. "The world you're in is bound to rub off on you. Just roll with it. Why would you have gone to the chair?"

"I woke up yesterday morning in a bare apartment on Murder Row with the cash and the jewels and a bloody knife in my hand."

"That sounds about right," Veronica said.

McElwee stopped and stared at her. "What do you mean?"

"That's a classic Turner-style opening. Grab the reader on page one with a dramatic predicament and a burning question, then rush the plot along so the reader is so busy trying to keep up, they can't think critically."

"I hate this place."

"I'm glad. Solve the crime, Joe, and we can leave. What's our next move?"

"Boss Harley."

"And how did you come to that conclusion?"

"What do you mean, how? All signs point to Harley. Who else would want to frame a cop? If Frump woke up with stolen jewels in his pocket, it's because someone put them there. Harley was on Murder Row yesterday morning with his crew. When they drove off from the diner, they were headed right toward The Loaded Arms. There's no way one guy could have cleared that place out in the time I was gone, but a crew of five? Sure. And who else would steal a cat? Only someone truly evil."

"Good work, Joe!"

Veronica put two fingers between her lips and let out an ear-splitting whistle. The Astor family Rolls responded to the call like an obedient dog.

"Back to the mansion?" asked the driver in his drawling English accent.

"No," said Joe, pulling the door shut behind him. "To Boss Harley's."

"Very good, sir. The hideout or the lair?"

Joe turned to Veronica with a questioning look.

"I don't know," she said. "What makes you think I have all the answers?"

"May I suggest the lair?" asked the driver. "The hideout is being repossessed due to unpaid taxes. It's crawling with revenue agents, and Mahstah Hahley avoids them like pickpockets."

"Ok, then," said McElwee. "The lair it is."

# 27

Boss Harley's lair was at the bottom of a scrub-covered canyon north of the city. The long dirt drive leading to the single-story ranch house was guarded by two dumb-looking thugs wearing army-issue trousers and stained wifebeaters.

One squatted in front of an army surplus Jeep, drawing circles in the dirt with the muzzle of a Colt 45. The other sat atop the Jeep's hood, a shotgun across his lap. They were talking. Neither noticed the silent Rolls prowling by.

"That's definitely Harley's place," said McElwee, pointing up the dusty drive toward the house. "There's the black Cadillac and the yellow Packard." Then to the driver he added, "Why don't you swing around back?"

The road looped around to the rear, ending at a shaded spot two hundred yards behind the house. The driver parked the Rolls between a pair of eucalyptus trees by the side of a dry stream bed.

A skinny, inbred-looking man sat on the post-and-rail fence that marked the edge of Harley's property, smoking a cigarette and eying the Rolls with bad intent. McElwee didn't like his sparse whiskers and weak chin, his dingy white t-shirt, or his beady, calculating eyes. He stepped out of the car anyway.

"I think yer in the wrong place, fella." The skinny gangster pulled the cigarette from between his narrow lips, spat a gushing load of tobacco juice into the dirt, then put the cigarette back.

"Now'd be a good time to turn around," he suggested, jumping down from the fence. His boots hit the dust with a thud, and he reached behind and pulled a revolver from the small of his back.

"Hear me?" he said.

Veronica stepped from the car just as McElwee was putting his hands up. The inbred startled at the sight of her.

"Hot damn!" He looked her up and down, cocked the trigger of his revolver, and said, "Now get on outta here, city boy. And leave the frail."

"Frail?" said Veronica in an unmistakable tone of affront. "Of all the stupid words for women those old crime writers came up with, frail was the worst!"

McElwee remembered coming across that word in a Raymond Chandler novel.

"Dame, I can accept," said Veronica, taking a step toward the gunman. "It's French for lady, and if you happen to mispronounce it, well, that just shows your ignorance."

"Quit with the words, lady." The inbred kept the gun on McElwee.

"And 'broad' I can accept," she said, stepping closer, and subtly motioning McElwee to do the same. "My shoulders are broad, and I'm broadly drawn, so I suppose the word is apropos."

"That's enough outta you." The gangster pointed his gun at her face, and when McElwee took two steps forward, the barrel pointed back toward him.

"But, frail? Do I honestly look frail to you? Hit him, Joe!"

"He has a gun!" said McElwee.

"Hit him!" cried Veronica.

"And get my brains blown out?"

The gunman was losing his patience. "Tell your dame to shut up, Joe."

"Why don't *you* tell me to shut up? If you're so tough and I'm so frail?"

"Now look, lady—"

Veronica cold-cocked him before he could finish his sentence. Laid him flat on his back in the dirt. Then she turned to McElwee and said, "Turnerverse. Any solid punch to the jaw results in a knockout. If the gun is pointed at a good guy, it won't go off. And then you finish it off with this." She bit her knuckles and dramatically shook the pain from her hand. "Now pick up his gun, Joe, and we'll go up to the house."

"I don't like guns," said McElwee.

"Then why do you have so many of them in your stupid book?"

She picked up the gun herself and then hesitated as she eyed the fence.

"What?" asked McElwee.

"I'm not sure how I'm going to get over that in this tight dress."

"The laws of physics haven't hindered the plot yet. Just jump it."

"I don't think I can. Do you mind giving me a hand?"

McElwee locked his fingers together, making a stirrup. She stepped in, he gave a little heave, and over she went. He followed a second later.

Dark scrub shielded the rear of the house, giving them cover on their approach. McElwee noticed Veronica's face was flushed. He couldn't decide whether she looked annoyed or just uncomfortable.

"Something bothering you?" he asked as they walked.

She shook her head, but he could tell by the way she bit her lip that she was lying.

"Tell me," he said.

"It's embarrassing," she whispered. "And keep your voice down. We're getting close enough for people to hear." She pointed toward an open window and said, "We'll sneak up there. Maybe we can eavesdrop."

"What's the matter?" he asked again.

"Shh. Let's get to the window."

They crept along the side of the house, then crouched low and kept their heads beneath the sill.

They could hear the voices inside clearly.

"So what's next, boss?" asked a man inside.

McElwee watched Veronica, wondering what had gotten into her. She kept clenching her left fist (the gun was in her right), scrunching her face, clamping her legs together, and gasping.

"Do you have to pee?" he asked.

"No. Shut up, ok?"

"Frump was the last decent cop in this town. Now that he's out of the picture, we got the run of the city," said a voice McElwee recognized as Boss Harley's. It was the same voice that had told him in front of the diner yesterday morning that Polski was the new guy being broken in.

"I knew it," McElwee whispered. "They framed Frump to get him out of the way."

"The only guy who can cause trouble now," Harley continued, "is Sternjaw, and I know how to take care of him."

Veronica let out a quiet gasp of annoyance. She clamped her legs tighter, scrunched her face, and rolled her hips uncomfortably.

"What in the world is wrong with you?" McElwee whispered.

"I'm horny as hell!"

"Now?" He looked around at the dust and scrub. "This is what turns you on?"

"No. I was reading erotica twenty-four-seven back at the bookshop, and then I wake up as this fertility goddess in the Turnerverse, where— Actually, I think it's Turner. He's never written a woman who *isn't* horny. God, I feel like I'm in heat! What a curse!"

"Well, I'm sorry. I can't do anything for you now. I'm with Dorothy."

"You couldn't do anything for me when you tried. You're a lover, not a lay, and you don't love me, so you have nothing to bring. Besides, I would never take you from her."

"Stop writhing!"

"I can't. What the hell did that pervert do to me? Oh my God, if I ever meet Niall Turner in person, I'm going to gouge his eyeballs out!"

"Try to focus," McElwee said as he inched away from her. "We're here to get clues, remember?"

"Argh!" Veronica groaned. He could feel her discomfort.

She slowly raised her head above the windowsill until she could see in. She motioned McElwee to do the same.

"Won't they see us?" he whispered.

"Does it matter? Just listen."

"But boss," said a little rat-faced henchman, "how are we gonna find Sternjaw?"

"I love the way they wait for our conversation to stop before they say something meaningful," Veronica said. "It makes the exposition so much more efficient."

"We don't gotta find him, Rat Face. We'll bring him to us," said Boss Harley.

"How?" asked a second henchman who seemed absurdly tall.

"Good lord, that Rat Face is ugly," Veronica whispered. "And the guy beside him, he must be seven feet tall."

"The plan's already in motion, Hightower," said Harley, picking up a skinny striped cat.

"Tabitha!" said McElwee. "Look how thin she is! She must not have eaten since yesterday."

Veronica shushed him.

"He'll come for his cat sooner or later," Harley said as he stroked the animal's back.

"I wouldn't do that," McElwee said softly. "She turns into a rabid polecat when she's hungry."

"And that'll be the end of Sternjaw!"

Another henchman, pale-skinned, with the ice-blue eyes of a killer said, "Can I off him, boss? I ain't offed nobody all week."

"He's all yours, Ice Blue. As soon as he shows up. Where's Polski?"

"Crying into his beer," said Ice Blue.

"Over that broad?"

"Yeah."

"Maybe you should off *him*," said Hightower, and Rat Face let out a high-pitched laugh.

Veronica turned to McElwee. "Do you notice anything off here?"

"Lots of things. But I sense you're referring to something in particular."

"Look at these guys," she said. "Every one of them is stupid and ugly. And then, look at the other men in this story: Frump, Walter, you. None of you are particularly attractive. Well, you, maybe, but just on the surface. Then look at Dorothy and me. We're both gorgeous in our own ways, are we not? And we're both available to you men. But what's available to us? Where's the prize we'd actually want to date?"

"You're just horny."

"That's part of what's driving me crazy. I'm horny, because Turner can't conceive of a woman who isn't horny, and there's not a single appealing man in the Turnerverse. The shower in my bathroom has a detachable head. That's the best I'm likely to do here."

"What about that guy?" McElwee pointed to a quiet henchman in the corner. He was young, twenty-five perhaps, clean and well groomed.

"*That's* my prize?" Veronica sounded underwhelmed.

"He's not hideous," said McElwee.

"Well there's a resounding recommendation! Anyway, he's a bad guy. He's on the wrong side."

"I thought women liked the bad boys."

"Young women, Joe. Despite what I look like here, in real life I'm forty-one. My minimum requirement for a man is that he earns his own beer money, and I'm not convinced the quiet kid in the corner is up to that."

"Yes," said Harley, walking toward the window with the cat on his shoulder. "I expect Sternjaw to show up any time now, and when he does—"

The cat interrupted him with a yowl and a quick triple-swat to the cheek that drew blood. Harley hurled the cat toward the window. She went through and McElwee caught her.

"Tabitha!"

"Rrrrr-now?"

"It's him!" cried Harley. "Sternjaw! Get him!"

Veronica and McElwee leapt to their feet and hightailed it back toward the Rolls. Harley was the first through the rear door, guns blazing, bullets kicking up dust around the legs of both protagonists.

The towering Hightower, the rat-faced Rat Face, and the cold blue-eyed killer, Ice Blue, were right behind their boss, firing away. The quiet kid with the good hygiene brought up the rear.

"Shoot!" cried McElwee as he ran toward the fence, Tabitha pinned by his left hand to his left shoulder. Two hundred yards had never looked so far.

"I can't," Veronica yelled. "I need both hands to hold up my boobs. These things are so impractical!"

A volley of lead whistled past her ears, pocking the dirt, the fence, and the eucalyptus trees ahead.

"Hold them up with one arm," McElwee said, panting. "Straight across, then shoot back over your shoulder with your gun hand."

She did as he said, rattled off four blind shots, and they heard four bodies thud to the ground behind them. They turned to look as they reached the fence. Harley lay in a lifeless heap fifty feet behind them. Next to him sprawled the gigantic Hightower. To his left, Rat Face. A few feet closer, Ice Blue, with a bullet in his heaving red chest, seemed about to breathe his last.

Only the young one remained. Veronica backed up to the fence as he approached, his gun pointed at her chest. McElwee wasn't sure, but he thought she was rubbing her behind against the fence. *Like an animal in heat.* Weren't those her own words?

"Are you gonna shoot me or what?" she asked the young man as McElwee dug the cat's claws from his shoulder.

The young man hesitated. McElwee sensed he had never shot a person before.

Ice Blue mustered his last ounce of energy to sit up. His gun six feet away in the dirt and out of reach, he tried to encourage the young man. "Plug her!"

"Would you *like* to plug me?" Veronica asked with a suggestive smile. McElwee thought her tone was inappropriate, given the life-and-death gravity of the situation. Her question sounded too much like an invitation. But he could also see she was struggling, squinting as if pained, clenching her fist, pressing her knees together like she had to pee.

The young guy hesitated and Ice Blue exhorted him once again. "Plug 'em both, Limbermember!"

"Limbermember?" Veronica sounded intrigued. "What kind of name is that?"

The young man shrugged. "I don't know. It's just a name. Like Hightower or Rat Face or Ice Blue. It doesn't mean anything."

"Are you sure?"

He didn't seem too sure.

"Get in the car," Veronica said.

And he did.

<h1 style="text-align:center">28</h1>

The next time McElwee saw her was at nine o'clock that evening, at the burger and beer joint where they had agreed to meet when they'd split up earlier. Lady Astor's driver had dropped Joe and Tabitha at 123 Terra, and then rounded the corner to drop Veronica and her new friend off at her house.

She looked relaxed now, smiling, glowing. She leaned over McElwee's shoulder, gave him a peck on the cheek, and dropped a copy of the evening paper on the bar in front of him.

"I hope you fed that poor starving pussy of yours," she teased.

"Tabitha's fine," he said, picking up the paper. "And you seem relieved."

"I like problems that have solutions. A meal is only as good as the appetite you bring to it, and I was famished, Joe. Famished, and then ravished, and now I'm famished again. I want a double cheeseburger and a pint of beer."

"Where's your new friend?"

"Who cares? He solved my problem, so I gave him bus fare and turned him loose. Turn the paper over, look at the bottom of page one."

He did. It showed a photo of Harley and his henchmen sprawled in the dirt. McElwee read the headline. "Boss Harley Offed by Frail."

The opening paragraphs described Boss's colorful criminal past. Veronica pointed at the subheading above paragraph six. "Assailant Had Colossal Rack and a Swell Pair of Gams."

"Where do you think they got that description?" McElwee asked.

"Probably from Ice Blue. The rest of them were dead. You know, in any other universe, they would have noticed my red hair, instead of fixating on my... Are you hungry?"

"I am, actually. I could go for a veggie burger."

"They don't have those in nineteen forty-eight. You'll have to order a burger with all the veggie toppings and no meat."

"Screw it then. I'll do the fish and chips."

"Ah. So you're a pescatarian."

They talked through the case as they ate. Veronica summarized the remainder of the article as it appeared on page three. The cops had found virtually all of the missing cash in Boss Harley's lair. They were comparing the serial numbers on the bills to the list Lady Astor had compiled.

They also found the jewels, which they could positively identify from photos the insurance company had taken when Lady Astor had bought her policy. All were accounted for, except the necklace and ring that the gang had planted in Frump's pockets.

"You were right," Veronica said. "It was Harley and his boys who cleaned out the apartment on Murder Row."

"And now the cops know," McElwee added, "that Harley framed Frump."

"And you were right about the press conference too," Veronica added. "That was a false ending back at the police station. It's actually one of Turner's more tired gimmicks. He throws the ending of one story into the middle of another, and then a few chapters later, he's like, 'Fooled ya! It's not really over.'"

"Yeah, well, I'll check in with Frump in the morning. It's been a long day, and I'd like to get to bed. And that crying guy behind us is really getting me down."

Veronica turned to look at the hunched man sobbing into his beer behind them.

"How long has he been crying like that?"

"Since before I got here. At least an hour. Hey, bartender! Check, please."

"That poor guy," Veronica said.

"Poor guy," McElwee repeated with sarcastic impatience. "Just about everyone's a pity case in the Turnerverse. Don't get sucked into other people's problems. Let's just wrap this case and get out of here."

"But, Joe, he's so sad! When's the last time you heard a man cry for a solid hour?"

"That was me," he said. "Reading the sales figures from my last literary novel." He read the bill, gave the bartender a ten, and told him to keep the change. "It's amazing how far a buck used to go. You ready to blow this joint?"

"Joe," whispered Veronica. "Look."

"What?"

She pointed to the belt line of the crying man's backside.

"Dorothy calls that a coin slot," said McElwee. "I'd never heard that one before."

"Read the name."

The black marker on the elastic band said Polski.

"Oh, Christ," said McElwee. "Not him again."

Veronica took a seat at the weeping man's side before McElwee could stop her.

"What's wrong, big fella?"

"Maureen will never love me," Polski blubbered.

McElwee remembered Ice Blue mocking Polski for crying into his beer over "some broad." Maureen must be the broad.

"Never is a very strong word," Veronica said.

"Not for me. I'll be dead any day now."

"And why is that?" Veronica asked.

McElwee gave up wanting to leave and took a seat at the table.

Eyeing him glumly, Polski said, "If I wasn't all blurry eyed, I'd blow your brains out. But I'm off duty tonight, so you'll have to wait till tomorrow. When's a good time to come by?"

"Wait," said Veronica. "Why will you be dead?"

"It's like Maureen keeps telling me. I'm a second-rate henchman. I got no backstory."

"Stop snarling," Veronica said.

"I can't. It's the only facial expression I have. That's another reason Maureen won't have me."

"What's backstory got to do with anything?" McElwee asked.

Veronica explained. "All the characters who make it from one volume to the next in a Turner series have backstory. He wants his readers to be invested, even in some of the bad guys. So he gives them a past. Not having backstory means you're not going to stick around. You're going to be part of the body count."

"I don't know what all that means," Polski said. "All I know is Maureen has the hots for Boss Harley, and he's got like, oodles of backstory."

"What *is* Harley's backstory?" McElwee asked. "He seemed reasonably intelligent. Why would he turn to a life of crime?"

"He flunked out of hairdresser school," said Polski.

"That's backstory?" McElwee was not impressed.

"It is in the Turnerverse," said Veronica. "On the one hand, readers can sympathize with him, because everyone has experienced that kind of disappointment. On the other hand, it gives them reason to hate him. If he knows what hurt feels like, why does he go around inflicting it on others?"

"Yeah, why?" Polski bawled.

"Look," said McElwee. He dropped the paper on the table and pointed to the photo of the dead Harley gang. "You're off the hook, Polski. Harley's dead."

Polski stared at the photo, read the headline three times, and asked as if in a stupor, "You mean I can go straight? Legit? No more gunfights?"

"I would take the opportunity if I were you," McElwee said. "Skip town. Go somewhere new. Start over. What kind of skills do you have?"

"I'm a piano mover. Licensed and bonded."

"Wait," said McElwee, "when you went to the Astor mansion the night of the murder, that was legit? You really were moving the piano?"

"Far as I know," Polski said.

"Harley didn't send you? You weren't casing the place?"

Polski shook his head. "Lady Agatha called me directly."

"You two were on a first-name basis?" asked Veronica.

Polski nodded. "The frame cracked on her Steinway and it could never be re-tuned. She was heartbroken. I drove two hours to pick up a matching model, same color concert grand. Same year and everything. That soothed her a little."

McElwee looked at Veronica. "This makes no sense. I thought Harley and his crew killed Lady Astor and planted the loot with me, so I would be framed. Then they planted some jewels on Frump to frame him. As Harley himself said, that rids LA of its two best investigators and gives him free rein to commit crimes. But if Harley didn't kill Lady Astor, then who did?"

"You got me," Veronica said.

McElwee and Veronica pumped Polski for more info. What time did the movers get there? What time did they leave? Who else was in the house?

But Polski couldn't tell them anything they hadn't already learned from Frump and Dorothy and Walter.

On their way out of the burger joint, McElwee told Veronica, "This really is a puzzler."

"One of the few things Turner does well," Veronica admitted, "is the red herring. He got us going down the wrong path, and we fell for it, hard."

## 29

Veronica showed up at the diner the next morning in a white sequined gown.

"A little over the top, don't you think?" asked McElwee. He was at the counter, drinking coffee and reading the morning paper.

"Turner didn't give me much to choose from. At this point, I wouldn't mind a pair of baggy sweats."

"You turned a lot of heads when you walked in here."

She rolled her eyes. "I'm so sick of that. Can we get a booth? I feel exposed up here in the open, like I'm on stage in front of a crowd that feels they have the right to gawk at me."

"Yeah, sure." McElwee stood and pointed toward a booth in the back.

"You know we can't get out of here," she said as they walked, "until we solve this case."

"Why not?" McElwee motioned her toward the side of the booth least visible from the counter. He took the other bench, facing the entrance.

"For the same reason people can't stop reading Turner's stupid books. Or any mysteries, for that matter. Once you get far enough into it, you have to know who did it."

"Well," said McElwee, "we just got another twist."

He pushed the paper across the table to her and pointed to the headline.

"Frump Dead in Wreck, Left Suicide Note."

"What?" Veronica read the article as the waitress handed McElwee a pair of menus. Veronica had finished reading by the time the young woman returned and poured their coffee.

"So the cops let him go," Veronica summarized, "because they figured out Harley framed him. He leaves the police station, gets into his car, and drives over a cliff. At his desk, the police chief finds a note. 'I'm sorry to have brought shame on this department. I can no longer live with myself.'

"What sense does that make, Joe? He'd been exonerated. Where's the shame in that?"

"Same thing I thought," said McElwee, eyeing the little fat man who'd just come through the door. "But I think there's a clue in there somewhere."

What was so strange about the little pug-faced man who'd just entered? He scanned the customers at the counter as if he was looking for someone. He had an extraordinary arrogance about him, staring right into people's faces. He didn't seem to care if he offended them.

"What is it, Joe? What are you looking at?"

"I have a bad feeling about this guy," McElwee said as the pugnacious ball of a man pushed his way through the tables, looking closely at every patron.

It struck McElwee all at once. What was odd about this guy, aside from his arrogant, overconfident manner, was his twenty-first-century clothing. The cargo pants, the white button-down shirt, and the Apple watch marked him as a man of Joe's own day and age. What was he doing here? And who was he hunting with such determined intensity?

Veronica turned to see what Joe was staring at. She shrieked when she saw him.

"Turner! Niall Turner!"

The man's eyes lit with sadistic enthusiasm at her cry. She stood and tried to run, but he was on her in a second, his stubby little fingers throttling her throat.

"Where's my *victim*?" he screamed. "Where's Suzette Holloway? You warned her, you little slut! You warned her, and she ran off!"

McElwee leapt from his seat and wrapped his arm around Niall Turner's throat from behind. He pushed his other arm against the back of the author's neck and began to squeeze. A sleeper hold, as the wrestlers used to call it.

"I have no victim," Turner croaked. "My psychopath got locked up before he had a chance to kill anyone, and now my novel is dead in the water! Where's Suzette? I have a fucking deadline here!"

McElwee put all his strength into the chokehold, and finally Turner was forced to let go. Veronica ran gasping through the exit, her hands clutching her bruised throat.

McElwee kept his hold on Turner even after Veronica escaped. The belligerent little pug was in serious difficulty now. McElwee felt the man's resistance slackening as his strength waned. Turner tapped McElwee's forearm like a spent cage fighter who'd had enough.

McElwee thought of what this man had done to Veronica's character, reducing a thoughtful, intelligent woman to a porn star in heat. He thought of how Turner had let the sensitive Dorothy languish in an insensitive world. And what about Suzette? It was bad enough this author couldn't provide a decent world for his creations. When he got bored, he killed them.

McElwee tightened his grip. He had decided to kill the man.

Then a new thought came to him. There had been hacks like Turner in decades past, writers whose lurid garbage topped the charts because they rode the latest trend, or because they had name recognition or a good publicist. Some of them had reached the top through sheer luck.

But garbage, over time, will be forgotten. It grows stale and the public demands newer, shinier garbage. Or at least, the publishers and film studios produce it, and the public accepts it.

Turner was not an author for the ages. A new generation of hacks was already beginning to replace him. His crappy writing would not survive him.

"If I kill him," McElwee thought, "his whole world goes down with him, including me. Including Veronica. We'll never get out of here. We'll just fade into darkness. We'll be dollar books on the table outside the bookshop, getting rained on, washed back into pulp."

He released the man.

Turner's eyes were watering and his face was purple. He tugged at his collar, gasping for air.

"Good man, Sternjaw." He put his hands on his knees and panted. "Way to jump to the defense of your frail. You overdid it though. Didn't you get that I was trying to cut the scene ten seconds ago, when I realized it had got away from me?" He made the tapping motion again. "It's called a tap out. It means stop. Come on, Joey, let's get a beer."

"It's eight a.m.," McElwee said.

"Alright, coffee then."

Turner loosened his tie and collar as they walked to the counter. A young woman poured two coffees into the cups in front of them. Turner leaned close to McElwee and said in a low voice that reeked of satisfaction, "You see the tits on that one?"

McElwee drew away and looked coldly at the man.

Turner tapped his chest and said proudly, "That's *my* work!"

"I never liked you, Niall."

"That's why I made you, Joey. You're better than me. I made you taller, better looking, and I gave you morals."

Taller? In his current incarnation, McElwee was five foot six. He took another look at Turner and estimated his height at five foot three.

"You see, Bronco Howitzer was six foot four," Turner explained. "He could beat the crap out of anyone, and he did. The critics started picking on me about that. I started losing the few female readers I had. Bronco's not real, they said. Bronco's one-dimensional. Solves every problem with his fists or his gun.

"Yeah, well, some problems need to be solved that way. If you don't like it, go read something else. Then I ran up against another problem. How many times can you recycle the same plot? My editor said eighteen, but I got thirty-two out of Bronco.

"Then I came up with you." He poked McElwee in the chest. "Joey Sternjaw. Handsome as all get-out. Dresses nice, solves problems with his brain. A real pussy magnet."

"There's no such thing as a pussy magnet," McElwee said.

"Oh, now don't be ungrateful," Turner warned. "See, I know something about women."

"I can't believe you even came out of one."

"Leave my mother out of this, Joey. See, I did some research. People say I don't do that, but I do. If I'm going to replace Bronco Howitzer with a new protagonist, I want him to appeal to the broadest possible audience. Women read more than men, and I had lost a lot of them at the end of the Bronco series.

"So I'm looking for a new guy. I ask myself what women like. I go read every women's magazine out there. *Cosmo, Allure, Glamour, Elle.*"

"That's your research?"

"Yeah, I'm thorough. Women like a guy who dresses sharp, has a little bit of depth, good moral character. That's how I came up with Sternjaw. You know, like, this guy isn't going to yield. He's gonna do what's right.

"And the best thing is, a guy like that doesn't have to chase the skirts. They come to him. You can thank me for Veronica. You can thank me for Dorothy."

McElwee wanted to punch him.

"Now look," said Turner, "I need you to tell me where Veronica lives."

"You don't know?"

"No. I farmed out the description of her pad to this little Chinese woman."

"The one who created Dorothy?"

"Yeah, Ming Wang."

It's Mae Chang, McElwee thought. But the man wasn't worth correcting.

"Where'd she put her? In Chinatown or something?"

"I don't know," McElwee said.

"Yes, you do."

"What do you want with her anyway?"

"First I'm gonna fuck her, and then I'm gonna kill her. She ruined my story."

"You're savage, Niall. You're the bottom of the barrel."

"Look," he said. "An author is like a mafia boss. He's gotta shepherd a bunch of characters through a plot. He has to maintain control. Any gets outta line, they have to go. As soon as the other characters see one broad's getting away with things without being punished, all hell breaks loose."

That was it, McElwee thought. That was the difference between the garbage Turner-like writing he himself had been cranking out lately and the more real piece he hadn't wanted to show anyone, the one that made Dorothy cry.

The writer didn't control the work any more than he controls the world he's reporting on. The best he can do is illuminate, and in that illumination, a feeling reader like Dorothy understands she's not alone. There's someone else out there who gets what she gets, another soul peering out from the darkness into a universe not of its own making.

When McElwee had first started writing, his stories used to happen to him. Now, like Turner, he was producing a product. There weren't a lot of Dorothys in the world—certainly not enough to pay the mortgage on the Turner mansion—but those were the ones worth writing for, the kindred souls searching for their tribe among the masses.

Veronica was as right about reading as she was about sex. The magic was in the connection.

"Don't worry," Turner said. "You don't have to tell me where she is. I'll find her."

McElwee watched him get up from the stool and walk out. He watched him walk the wrong way down the sidewalk, away from Veronica's house. When the little man was out of sight, McElwee went to the payphone near the entrance. He pulled Veronica's card from his pocket, the one she'd left with Dorothy, and dialed her number.

It rang six times, then ten, then twenty, before he remembered there was no such thing as voicemail in 1948.

McElwee hung up and wondered what to do next.

Go to her house? What would he do then? Hide her? Where? It would be pointless to take her to his place. Surely Turner knew where Joey Sternjaw lived. He would know the Astor mansion as well. And McElwee knew that asking Dorothy to help Veronica was pushing it.

Best just to stay away from her for now, he decided. If I went to her house, the brute would probably follow me right to her.

God, I wish Frump was still here. I need a right-hand man. But Frump was a Turner creation. He probably would have been loyal to his author.

Who can help me then? Walter? He's too shallow to be good for anything.

Manuel? Gunsel? They're not fully drawn enough.

Dorothy had the brains to help, but after Turner told him his plans for Veronica, McElwee didn't want to risk putting Dorothy anywhere near the beast.

Who did that leave?

Then it hit him. Henchman don't cry. Polski was getting away from his author, developing feelings and thoughts of his own. He was too minor a character for Turner to notice, or else Turner would have reined him in, put the snarl back on his face, and sent him out to kill. Polski was big and strong, he was too far under Turner's radar to be noticed, and he had a Tommy gun.

McElwee picked up the vinyl-bound directory hanging from the pay phone. Opening the Yellow Pages, he flipped to the letter P, then to Piano Movers, and ran his finger down the page. Big Dumb Polack Piano Movers had an office in Burbank. Stanislav Polski, proprietor. They opened at nine a.m.

30

McElwee's cab rolled up just in time for him to see Polski shutting the twin rear doors of his moving truck. Amazing, he thought, that they were actually able to move pianos in those things. The cargo bay was barely big enough to hold a Steinway grand, and it didn't have the automatic lift he was used to seeing on the back of modern box trucks. Loading and unloading that vehicle required brute strength and a steady hand.

"Polski!"

Polski turned to see McElwee exiting the cab.

"What are you doing?"

"Leaving," Polski answered, "like you said. It's time for a new start. I can't drum up enough business around here to stay afloat. That's why I was moonlighting as a thug."

"You still have that Tommy gun?"

"Yeah, why?"

"How would you like to stick it to the man?"

"What man?" Polski looked confused.

"The one who didn't give you any backstory."

"You mean there's a man responsible for that?" Polski clenched his fist and began to snarl.

"That's the spirit," said McElwee. "Go get the gun."

"Where we going?"

"West Hollywood."

McElwee figured it was safe to roll around his and Veronica's neighborhood in a moving truck. Turner wouldn't be looking out for one of those. And though the author might expect to find Joey Sternjaw with Dorothy or Veronica, Polski would never even occur to him. He hadn't even paid attention to the character when he created him. Turner had apparently

160

reached a scene where he needed a big dumb thug, a throwaway with muscles, so he put a snarl on the guy, turned him loose, and forgot about him.

McElwee's only trip to Burbank had come in 2022, when he visited LA at the behest of a fellow writer. He'd been looking into scriptwriting opportunities for an HBO series, but the collaborative writing process intimidated him. He didn't like sitting around a table with a bunch of other writers, throwing out ideas and watching them get shot down, then watching as ideas he thought were stupid get spun up by inspired minds into good dialogue and compelling action.

He had left LA feeling like an impostor, a wannabe writer who needed to prove himself, and he had gone back home and proved himself the wrong way. The LA experience was one of the final steps on the long road to his selling out. He noted now, with bitterness and regret, that the Turnerization of his writing was born from a feeling of inadequacy rather than strength. Jealous of the success of others, of the scriptwriters and the Turners and the entire *New York Times* bestseller list, he had tried to prove he could be someone he didn't even want to be.

"You always just sit and stare like that?" Polski asked, turning to look at him from the driver's seat.

"I'm thinking."

"About what?"

"How much better this city looks in nineteen forty-eight. It doesn't have the strip malls yet. The Seven-Elevens and tacky nail salons and big box stores."

Polski looked at him. "I have no idea what you're talking about."

"And I didn't either for a long time, but I'm starting to get it. Hey, pull over up at the corner. I want to use that phone."

"I also like to think," Polski said as he brought the truck to a halt. "About kielbasa, and beer, and broads, and gams."

McElwee put his hand on his companion's shoulder. "It's not your fault, Stan."

"I don't mind it."

"Because you don't know any better. If I had written you, who knows? Maybe you'd be playing the pianos instead of moving them. You have a nickel?"

"Yeah, sure." Polski pulled a coin from his pocket and flipped it to McElwee.

At the phone, McElwee pulled Veronica's card from his pocket and was about to drop in his nickel before thinking better of it. She wouldn't risk going home. She knew Turner would eventually find his way there.

Joey Sternjaw, McElwee thought, would have an office downtown. A heavy wooden desk with an old-fashioned blotter. A swivel chair and an old steel fan and slatted blinds that sliced the sunlight into sharp lines accentuating the curves of his desperate female clients.

He would have a secretary too. Never mind that a private detective in LA could barely bring in enough income for one. Turner would give his dick—the word made McElwee cringe—a supple young secretary, a hot one he could hook up with on the side when business was slow.

Veronica, sharp reader that she was, would know this. In this age before voicemail, she would look up his office number in the Yellow Pages, call, and leave a message with his secretary.

McElwee opened the book. Under Private Detectives, he found a note saying "See Private Investigators." He flipped ahead and found a quarter-page ad. "Joey Sternjaw, the dick you want."

He dialed the number and a woman picked up on the second ring.

"Sternjaw Detective, how may I help you?"

"Hey um..." McElwee realized he didn't know the name of his assistant-slash-paramour, so he just said, "Babe."

"Joey? Where have you been? I've been worried sick!"

"I've been busy, Babe. Lots going on."

"I missed my period!"

"Christ, this is *not* the time!"

"Well when is the time, Joey? That's what I'd like to know. It's never *the time* with you! You've been stringing me along for years!"

"Look, I want to know if anyone called and left a message for me." In the back of his mind, he imagined how Niall Turner would get his detective out of this mess with his secretary. Probably take her out for a nice dinner, buy her a trinket, and screw her again. She'd get her period in the morning, and they'd be all patched up.

The secretary, he thought, might be better off with Polski. He wasn't a handsome man, but at least he cared enough to cry.

"Yes," she said. "As a matter of fact, I just hung up with some hysterical woman a few seconds before you called."

"She say where she was?"

"In the back of a laundromat at La Cienega and Waring. She said a guy named Turner was trying to kill her."

"Damn!" said McElwee.

"Oh, and Dorothy called. She wants to see you at her house right away."

"One thing at a time," he said.

McElwee hung up and jumped back into the truck.

"To La Cienega and Waring, pronto!"

Polski hit the gas.

## 31

The red block letters above the laundromat's plate glass windows said Yamaguchi, but McElwee recognized the greeting of the woman at the register—*Ni Hao*—as Chinese.

Then came the startle of recognition. He hadn't seen Mae Chang in four years. How did she get in here? Turner knew her. She had ghostwritten for him once. She must have seeped in through the author's subconscious.

What a joy to see her! Possibly the brightest and most creative mind he'd ever met.

"You want massage?" she asked in a sharp Chinese accent. "Lo mein? Starch in shirt?"

Oh God, thought McElwee. What the hell did Turner do to her?

He asked if a man and woman had been in recently.

"Horrible oaf want to make baby without consent!" the woman blurted, pointing toward the rear of the store. "Boob lady need help!"

McElwee could hear the sounds of a scuffle coming from the back room.

"Come on!" He grabbed Polski by the arm, pulling him and his machine gun toward the rear of the building.

"He not get her yet," called the proprietor. "She a feisty one!"

McElwee drove his shoulder into the door full speed, then bounced backwards onto his ass on the linoleum floor.

"Look, this is how it works," said Polski patiently, turning the knob. He gently nudged the door open to the sound of Veronica's shrieks.

McElwee leapt to his feet and charged into the room behind Polski. He lunged at Turner, pushing him against the side wall, the two of them nearly tripping over a sack of freshly washed towels.

Turner clipped McElwee's jaw with a right uppercut, a glancing blow. McElwee responded with a left that missed. Veronica fled into Polski's arms.

For the next minute or so, the two authors did their best to trade blows, but almost every punch they threw missed. Finally, they both doubled over, winded.

"That was pathetic," Turner said. "Absolutely pathetic fight scene."

"That's what happens in the real world when two out-of-shape, middle-aged guys go at it," said McElwee.

"When did the real world start appearing in my work?"

"When she showed up." McElwee pointed back toward Veronica. "Shoot him, Polski!"

"Shouldn't you get out of the way first?" Polski asked.

"Nah. Just snarl and shoot."

Polski's lip turned up in an ugly display of anger, and he sprayed a hundred bullets in the direction of the authors.

When the gun emptied out, McElwee checked his suit for holes. There were none.

"Remember?" he said to Turner. "In the Turnerverse, good guys don't get hit with that kind of spray. But you..." He pointed to a tear in Turner's pants, just above the knee. "You got a scratch there. You're going to need a Band-Aid."

"What?" cried Turner. "I'm a bad guy?"

"Looks like it," McElwee said.

Turner looked in horror at the reddening scratch. "My God, I'm bleeding! Call a doctor! Call an ambulance! Somebody call the universe! Niall Turner is bleeding!"

"Come on," said McElwee. "Let's get out of here."

## 32

As the moving truck made its way southwest on Pico Boulevard, McElwee asked Veronica what had happened.

"He caught me outside a liquor store on La Cienega," she said. "It sucks, having hair like this, a figure like this. You can spot me a mile away. I ran, but he chased me into the laundromat. That man is so disgusting! Ew! Ew! Ew! I need to wash him off me."

"What, uh..." McElwee was afraid to ask. "What did he do?"

"When he finally cornered me, he buried his head in my boobs, called me mommy, and asked me to spank him. I told you that man has issues."

McElwee was relieved to learn no serious harm was done during the attempted assault.

Now Polski chimed in. "Where we going, boss?"

"To the LAPD wrecking yard. And don't call me boss."

"Sure thing, boss."

"Shouldn't you be checking in with Dorothy?" asked Veronica.

McElwee gave her a funny look.

"What?" she asked.

"Yeah," said McElwee. "I should. My secretary said she wanted to see me."

"So why are you looking at me like my question was off-base?"

"Because there's no way you could have known the secretary told me that. Seems like another one of Turner's information leaks."

"I have no idea what transpired between you and your secretary. I'm just speaking as an avid reader. Dorothy is my favorite character in the Turnerverse, and she's been gone a long time. You think she'll ever like me?"

McElwee shook his head. "Not in this triangle. It's not in the cards."

"Well that sucks. Because I think we'd be friends under different circumstances."

"Hey, Polski, turn left up here." McElwee pointed toward the chain-link fence of a wrecking yard.

Inside the fence, the driver of a flatbed truck was dumping the remains of a mangled green Ford onto the asphalt. A uniformed officer stopped them at the gate.

"What's up, Sternjaw?"

"I was just about to ask you the same question. Is that Frump's Ford?" McElwee pointed to the crumpled green wreck.

"Pulled it out of a canyon near the Palisades about an hour ago. It went over sometime last night."

"Mind if I have a look inside?" McElwee asked.

"If you're into that sort of thing," the cop replied.

McElwee climbed out of Polski's truck and walked to the dark green wreck. Veronica followed.

McElwee ducked his head through the driver's window and examined the steering wheel, the dash, and the seat. Veronica turned away.

"I can't stand gore," she said. "Not even the description of it."

"Take a look," McElwee said.

"No. I hate those authors who rub your nose in blood and suffering."

"Open your eyes," McElwee said. "Look inside."

She hesitated for a moment, and then decided to trust him.

"Where's the blood?" she asked.

"Where's the dent in the steering wheel?" asked McElwee, in a knowing tone. "If his head didn't hit the top of it, his chest would have hit the middle and crushed it in. The wheel's intact. This car was empty when it took the plunge."

He walked back to the cop guarding the gate.

"Where's the body?" McElwee asked.

"In the morgue," said the cop. "The autopsy's pretty much a formality. Frump was thrown from the car and incinerated. The friction of going through the windshield must have lit him like a match. The impact knocked out all his teeth and the fire burned off his finger prints. The only way they could identify him was by the badge and intact driver's license found beside the body."

McElwee and Veronica gave each other a knowing look.

On the drive to the Astor mansion in Beverly Hills, McElwee wondered aloud what it would be like to live in a universe where the cops could be hoodwinked by such a trick. Or where the friction of passing through a windshield would actually set a person on fire.

Veronica, possibly thinking along the same lines, let out a sigh as Polski kept a steady foot on the accelerator, and the truck rumbled up the hill.

# 33

They found Dorothy pacing anxiously in the entryway just inside the door. When she saw McElwee, she threw her arms around his neck and kissed his cheek.

Her look of relief melted to disdain when she saw Veronica.

"What is *she* doing here? Have you no class, Joey? Bringing that tramp right to my door?"

"Tramp?" Veronica seemed genuinely wounded.

"Relax," said McElwee. "She needs a shower."

"I'm sure she does, but I don't want that woman taking off her clothes in my house."

"Let her use Walter's shower at least," said McElwee. "Turner's been at her."

"Who is Turner?" Dorothy looked Veronica up and down as if in search of damage.

"An awful, awful man," said Veronica.

"I suppose you have to put up with a lot of those in your line of work," Dorothy said acidly.

"Why, you little—"

Polski and McElwee grabbed Veronica before she could get her hands around Dorothy's throat.

"Take her to a shower," McElwee said, relinquishing Veronica to Polski. "Upstairs or wherever." As he watched them leave, he said to Dorothy, "It's a shame you two can't get along."

"Joey, what took you so long? I left a message with your secretary hours ago."

"I was busy," McElwee said.

"With *her* again? Veronica? You said you weren't going to touch her."

"And I didn't. I just had to get her away from Turner."

"Who is this Turner you keep talking about?"

"You ever wonder why you're so lonely and unfulfilled?"

"Joey! What a thing to say! Have you lost your manners too?"

"It's because of Turner. He made this place."

Dorothy looked up at the ceiling, down at the walls. "The house? He must be very old. This house was built decades ago."

"This world," McElwee said. "And everything in it. Except you. You ever feel like you don't belong here?"

"You know I do, Joey. But I don't go blaming it on others. That's a sure way to lose in life. We're each responsible for ourselves, and we have to do our best to make the life we want."

"You have no chance here."

"Enough of this, Joey. I called you here for a reason. Come with me."

He followed her upstairs, past Walter's room and hers, to the window at the end of the hallway. She looked out over the yard.

"What are you looking for?" McElwee asked.

"Walter and his friends. They're not in the pool, and I don't think they're in the house. The Rolls is out front, and so is Walter's Cadillac. They're around here somewhere."

She squinted, put her hand above her eyes, and leaned closer to the window.

"Is the garden shed shaking?"

McElwee took a look. "I believe it is. Swaying side to side."

"Ok, then, they're busy. Come in here."

She led him into Walter's room, where Polski lay on the pink heart-shaped bed reading a celebrity tabloid. They could hear the shower running in the attached bathroom.

"This way," said Dorothy. She led him to a walk-in closet filled with men's suits, ties, and shoes.

"You see this?" asked Dorothy. "I don't know what's gotten into Walter the past few days, but he dumped his whole foppish wardrobe and now he dresses like a man. He cut his hair too, and toned down the queen act. He seems happier. But that's not what I wanted to show you. Look at this."

She pointed to a steamer chest large enough to hold McElwee's entire wardrobe five times over.

"It arrived this morning. Walter took it from a deliveryman at the front door. I was walking past, in the hall. I asked him what it was. He said he'd take care of it. I know that tone, Joey. When a man doesn't want you to look at something."

McElwee recalled that in the few early Turner books he did read, the essential women—the ones who survived for more than a few chapters and had meaningful dialogue—were always nosey. He used to think it was a stereotype reflecting Turner's shallow understanding of women.

Then, when he himself started writing Turner-like mysteries, he realized how handy a woman's nosiness could be. She could dig into things the detective might not have access to, surfacing clues as he sensed Dorothy was about to do now.

"Walter and Manuel and Gunsel hustled this upstairs as fast as they could. And look." She pointed to the address written on top.

Lada Agatha Astor<br>
Casa Incognita<br>
Cancun, Mexico

"I opened it," Dorothy said. "It's filled with her favorite clothes. Then I started making calls to all the shipping companies in town. It took six tries, but I found the one that had delivered this. They said they couldn't get it through Mexican customs because of the jewelry inside. There were no papers proving ownership, and the customs officers said they couldn't risk admitting stolen goods into the country. Not without a bribe. The shippers had no bribe money so they brought it back.

"I asked them over the phone when this trunk had been sent, and by whom. They told me it was Gram. She sent it the day before she died."

Dorothy looked at McElwee. "Now what do you make of that, Mister Detective?"

McElwee didn't miss a beat. "You told me that on the night of the murder, you looked into the library and saw Lady Astor lying on the floor in a pool of blood. Did you check to see if she was alive?"

"I couldn't go near her, Joey. It was too gruesome. I told you that."

"So you never actually verified she was dead?"

Polski entered then and said Veronica wanted a change of clothes. "She said she ain't gonna wear no more of the sexpot stuff. She's tired of people ogling her."

"I have nothing that would fit her," Dorothy said. "Take something of Walter's."

Polski picked out a pair of baggy pinstriped trousers and a freshly pressed Oxford shirt.

Dorothy and McElwee waited for him to leave before resuming their conversation.

"So your Gram gets stabbed," McElwee said, "and Frump responds to the call. You don't know for sure your Gram is dead, but Frump doesn't say otherwise, so you just roll with that."

"And now Frump is dead too," Dorothy said. "Did you see this morning's paper?"

"Frump's not dead, and neither is Lady Astor. You said he'd been here earlier in the evening, having tea with your Gram."

"Oh, Joey, surely you're not suggesting..."

"You did say they got along."

"Yes, but Gram is eighty-one."

"So? When two people fake their own deaths, it's not coincidence. You know anything about this Casa Incognita?"

"I called our travel agent. She said it's a discreet high-end resort for rich people who want to disappear."

"Call her back," McElwee said. "Tell her we need four tickets on the next flight to Cancun. And a cat carrier."

"Who has a cat?"

"I do."

McElwee had Polski stop at 123 Terra on the way to the airport so he could collect Tabitha.

Veronica, wearing Walter's baggy suit, knew why. Dorothy, though she might have been curious, wouldn't ask. She hadn't spoken since they got into the moving van. After McElwee had refused to hear her objection to Veronica's presence, she made him sit between them.

"I'm not rubbing shoulders with *her*," she had said under her breath, in an unmistakably angry tone.

Polski was the one who finally put the question to him. "Why are you bringing your cat to Mexico?"

"Because when we wrap this case, we can get out of here and go back to the real universe. I want her with me when I get home."

Veronica looked annoyed. McElwee had committed a gaffe akin to breaking the fourth wall in theater. The characters weren't supposed to know they were in a story, much less that there might exist some other universe in which writers created and readers consumed them.

Dorothy might have asked what he meant by this "real universe," but she looked tense and irritated. She sat with her arms folded tightly over her chest, eyes fixed defiantly forward. McElwee felt she had every reason to be annoyed, given Veronica's presence and his own strange behavior.

Polski didn't follow up either, quietly absorbing the tension around him like a child on a road trip with parents who weren't talking to each other.

Veronica leaned in toward McElwee and whispered, "Use the Elmore Leonard trick. Please?"

McElwee nodded to indicate he understood.

# 34

"I don't understand how we got here so fast," said Polski. "One minute, we're in LA, and the next, Cancun."

Dorothy, Veronica, and McElwee scanned the grounds of the luxurious seaside hideaway for signs of Lady Astor. Casa Incognita, a massive Italian-style villa with a terra-cotta roof, was surrounded by lush gardens and verdant walkways.

"Thank you," Veronica said softly to McElwee. "The tension in that van was awful. There's no way I could have endured eight hours of that on a nineteen-forties passenger plane."

The Elmore Leonard trick was one McElwee hadn't learned until he started writing Turner-style mysteries. An interviewer had once asked Leonard how he kept his stories moving at such a fast clip. The author had a simple explanation. "I leave out the parts readers skip."

The long flight would have been boring, with McElwee trying to play peacemaker between Dorothy and Veronica, while Polski snored loudly and the cat complained. Much better just to show up in Mexico refreshed, he thought.

"Gram!" cried Dorothy.

And there she was, the supposedly dead Lady Astor, in the flesh just up ahead.

McElwee watched Dorothy run toward her Gram with the enthusiasm of a schoolgirl and the grace of an athlete.

The old woman was dressed in white. Frump walked beside her, dressed in the only rumpled brown suit he owned.

Veronica, Polski, and McElwee followed slowly, unwilling to exert themselves in the sultry heat, and not wanting to intrude on the reunion of Dorothy and her beloved grandmother. They watched as the two women hugged, and caught up just as they began to speak.

"Why, Gram? Why would you leave me like that, thinking you were dead?"

"Sorry, hon. I just had to get out."

The woman's voice was harsher than McElwee expected. In the press photos, she always looked so elegant. To hear her talk, you'd think she'd spent her life boozing and smoking. Dorothy had told him Gram liked Frump's tales from the street. Maybe the stories captivated her because she was inwardly suited to that rough life she didn't get to live.

"Heya, Joey!" Frump seemed genuinely happy to see his old friend.

"Frump," said McElwee flatly, not even pretending to share his enthusiasm. The two shook hands.

"Don't hold it against me, Joey. Edna was miserable. All she's done these past twelve years is stand at the ironing board and wring her hands. She'll be better off back in Buffalo with her mom. Believe me."

"Was Walter in on this?" Dorothy asked.

Gram nodded.

"But why?"

"We've been extorting each other for years," Gram said. "I was on to him the day you two married. Caught him in the bathroom with Manuel. I wasn't going to say anything at first. I had enjoyed Manuel's services myself."

"Gram!"

"Don't look so surprised, Dottie. Your mother was a spark plug just like me. You come from a long line of them. You just haven't hit your groove yet."

"Gram, love is sacred!"

"All you prissy romantics say that. One day, you'll run into a guy like Frump here." She motioned her thumb toward the dowdy detective. "He's not much to look at, but wait till you get him in the sack. He burns the house down every time!

"The problem is, he's fifty-six. Practically still in diapers. If there's one thing Hollywood hates more than a fairy, it's a cougar. Walter understood that. He threatened to out me for molesting young Frump. I threatened to out him for his antics with Manuel."

Walter as he was originally drawn, thought McElwee, didn't need much outing. Turner had made sure there'd be no mistake about which way Dorothy's husband swung.

"Finally, we came to an agreement," Gram continued. "I'd go, Walter would stay. He got the house, I got the fortune. And the dynamo here." She smiled at Frump.

"So you staged this?" Dorothy sounded incredulous. "You staged your own death? I would never in a million years have guessed you capable of such a thing!"

"Yeah, yeah." Gram waved her off. "I played my part well enough, the stodgy old dowager. Good riddance to that! Now I can finally *live*."

"But why?" Dorothy asked. "You were rich, you had a mansion high in the hills. You didn't have to follow anyone's rules. Certainly if Walter could carry on as openly as he did, you could too. So why, Gram? Why run away?"

"Because I needed a plot!" screamed a voice behind Dorothy.

They all turned at once to look at him. Turner's face was red from the heat, or from anger, or both. The young man standing beside him was very good looking, McElwee noted, and also very scary. There was something chilling in his eyes, a hole deep enough to silence the screams of even his most terrified victims.

"Nothing moves without a plot," Turner screamed. He was nearly in a rage. He directed his next outburst at Veronica. "The plot you *ruined* when you warned that waitress to skip town."

He looked her up and down, his sour face showing disapproval of her men's slacks and Oxford shirt.

"What?" he scoffed. "You had a bad experience with a man, and now you've gone dyke on me?"

"How dare you speak to her that way!" said Dorothy.

"She ruined my story," Turner said. "But no worries. I sprang my psycho from the clink in LA and gave him a new knife. All he needs now is a victim. And you'll do just fine. The willowy little rich girl pining away in her castle. The flat-chested princess with all the precious feelings. How'd you like to slit that throat, Chester?"

The young man's eyes glinted with delight.

"Bet she bleeds like a champ," Turner said.

"You horrid little man!" Dorothy stepped forward and slapped him.

"Ha!" chuckled Turner, putting his hand to his cheek. "Your frail little patsy-slap feels like foreplay. Do it again, you'll give me a hard-on."

Dorothy cold-cocked him with a right to the jaw and he went over backwards. He was out before he hit the ground.

"Turner has to remember his own rules," Veronica whispered to McElwee. "That one was right on the chin."

McElwee noted with pleasure that Dorothy did not put her knuckles in her mouth or shake out her hand after the punch.

"That's class," he whispered to Veronica. "She doesn't have to overdo it." Then to Frump, he added, "Shoot him."

"The psycho?"

"Yeah," said McElwee. "The guy is obviously nuts. Go ahead and pump a couple rounds into his chest."

The young psychopath snarled defiantly as Frump emptied his service revolver. Each bullet caused him to stagger dramatically, but he didn't fall until the last one hit.

"Boy, he was a bad one," Frump said. "He took six bullets and kept on lurching. I think he was trying to get out some kind of monologue."

Veronica leaned down and reached into Turner's pocket as he started to come to.

"What are you doing?" asked Lady Astor.

"Taking his pen. So he can't write his way out of this."

"Wait," said Dorothy. "What is that noise?"

McElwee heard it too. A steady beeping. Polski, Frump, Veronica, and Lady Astor all looked around them, trying to find the source of it.

Veronica gave him a knowing look, explaining in a glance what they both knew about the genre. The mystery had been solved, the bad guys got their comeuppance, the shooting of the two-dimensional psycho was the money shot in the orgy of good guy versus bad guy moral porn. The story was over.

*Beep. Beep. Beep.*

"Joey!" exclaimed Dorothy. "What's happening to you?"
What *was* happening to him?
The world was going black. Everything and everyone in it was fading.
"Joey!" Dorothy grabbed his wrist. "Joey, don't leave me!"
"Dorothy!"
The beeps got faster and louder, and then he heard a new voice. A different woman, familiar but out of place.
"He's waking up," said the voice.
"Joey!" Dorothy's voice rang faint and distant as the world continued to fade. "Joey, wait!"
"Dorothy!"
And then the other woman: "Should I get the nurse?"
Dawn was coming. A pale light.
And the woman who asked if she should get the nurse said, "Joe? How are you feeling?" She was holding his hand, kneading it gently. And then the beeps of the hospital monitors rang shrill in his ear and the harsh fluorescent light stung his eyes, and Veronica Wentworth with her oversized glasses and her mop of black frizz loomed over him with a smart-alecky expression.

"Well, look who's back in the world of the living! You gave me quite a scare there, Joe. Why can't you watch where you walk?"

His head throbbed with pain, and he must have made a face, because Veronica's look softened, and she said, "Sorry. I shouldn't tease you till you're better, and I hope that's soon, because I have a lot to say about that dumb-ass book you wrote."

He didn't like the way she looked at him, with her long thin nose and her unblinking owl eyes that seemed to see everything at once and seemed to always know which question to ask. In that moment, he was a book and she was reading him without his consent and there was nothing he could do about it.

She gave him a curious look and she said, "That name you kept repeating before you woke... Who is Dorothy?"

# McElwee Makes His Choice

# 35

He left the hospital after two days and drove the two hours from Veronica's small town to his basement apartment, his head pounding the whole way. At first, he didn't believe the doctor's warning that the headache and the mental fog would continue for several days.

"After that type of concussion," said the neurologist, "you can't undertake anything that requires sustained focus. Not for at least another week."

The drive proved the doctor right. McElwee had to stop twice to close his eyes and rest his mind. As he parked in front of his apartment, the relief of arriving home melted into dread at having to inhabit that damp basement flat once again.

He descended the steps, wet with mold, ducked beneath the brick overhang, and leaned on the old wood door to catch his balance, another thing that was off since the concussion. He took a couple of breaths as he steadied himself and found his keys. The click of the sliding deadbolt echoed inside the apartment and he went in.

Why was it so cold inside? He forgot; he had turned down the heat to save money.

He tossed his keys on the table beside the door. They skidded off and clattered to the floor, the sound shooting through his brain like shattering glass.

He pulled off his old coat, dropped it on the floor, and headed to bed.

From the bathroom—what was that stench? That horrid smell?

The litter box!

Then came a sharp pain as claws dug into his ankles and teeth sank into his Achilles tendon. Tabitha! Twelve hours without a meal made her savage. He'd been gone three days.

He turned and headed to the kitchenette, dragging that cat with him, her claws still attached to his pants leg.

"Sorry, Babe. I didn't know I'd be gone that long."

He checked the cabinet. No cat food. He opened the fridge and saw the remains of a whole chicken he'd bought from the hot shelf at the supermarket the night before he left. The store let it go for half price at ten p.m., after it had been drying under the heat lamp since noon. Still in the poverty mindset, McElwee had calculated it as three days of cat food for three dollars and fifty cents. He couldn't *not* buy it.

"Here, cat." He dropped the carcass on the floor and watched his tabby's tail curl into a question mark as it sniffed the dead bird.

"I'm going to sleep."

He left to the sound of the cat's contented purr.

# 36

The next morning, McElwee sat propped in bed in a wool sweater and hat, with a mug of steaming tea on the nightstand, his computer on his lap and Tabitha curled at his feet. Rain pattered in the window well beside his bed. A rolled-up towel pressed into the crack between sill and sash absorbed the runoff that would normally trickle in. His head still ached and he dreaded reading the final writing assignments from his two undergrad classes.

He had given a cursory glance to a dozen or so papers, scanning the opening paragraphs to find the usual subjects. A coming-of-age story, a dystopian fantasy about a band of teenagers who survived the apocalypse, two tales of first love, a boy bonding with dad over the restoration of a 1968 Corvette, a superhero action adventure, something about cinnamon muffins being a metaphor for the soul, a sci-fi story about a kid who couldn't tell if he was an artificial intelligence inside someone's smart watch or an actual kid, and a handful of clunky allegorical tales: one anticapitalist, one anticolonial, and two blasting the patriarchy.

Oh, God, he thought. Please get me another life!

Then he remembered and his face brightened. Open the bank website. Log in. Check the balance.

His heart leapt at the numbers. Sixty-one thousand currently available, plus a pending deposit of 154,000.

I'm not even going to read those papers, he thought. They all get A's, except that kid who never runs spell-check.

He opened a new browser tab, went to the artificial intelligence chatbot he'd bookmarked, and typed in a prompt:

*Give me thirty-one ways of saying this is a brilliant paper, you're a genius, and you have a bright future.*

He cut and pasted the results into the student evaluation app and finished his tea.

Then he opened the word processor and began composing his resignation letter. He'd need to send two copies, one to each of the schools that had employed him.

How to begin? He scratched his chin as he mulled it over. Should he mention the schools' shirking of their core mission? How they were churning out kids who lacked critical thinking skills? How about their refusal to pay a living wage to the lowly adjunct professors teaching the subjects the schools supposedly valued so deeply? How about their refusal to provide health insurance? How about the fact that neither he nor any of his disposable colleagues ever knew until the last minute how many classes they'd be teaching, and thus how much money they'd earn? How the hell was anyone supposed to plan a life without a stable income?

The old Joe McElwee, literary Joe, would have had a field day with this assignment, pouring his grievances into a thirty-page screed condemning the academic system, mindless consumerism, and the rotting morals of the social elite.

Writing for the mass market, however, had taught him to be more succinct.

*Dear Bastards,*
*I quit.*

# 37

The day before he was to leave for New York to negotiate a new publishing contract, he forced himself to read through the story he'd written, the tale of his failed marriage that had so moved the lovely Dorothy Astor. He read it three times, as he had promised himself. And then he was going to burn it, exorcise that chapter of his life and move on. That had been the plan, anyway.

But something had shifted. Maybe it was Veronica asking him to be true to himself in that long, strange dream of 1948. Or maybe that blow to his head had rattled something loose in his brain, something that had been stuck for years.

The story hurt less on the second reading, and on the third, he felt tremendous compassion for both Leanne and himself. Sure they were awful to each other. They were awful to themselves. But their problems hadn't arisen from nowhere. They didn't just sit down one day and say to themselves, I'm going to be a rotten spouse, and a drinker, and a philanderer. I'm going to be crabby and hot-headed and sleep with people I don't know and wake up sick in unfamiliar places.

No. Their problems came from seeds planted long ago, from patterns of thought and behavior they had failed to examine, from real wounds and perceived slights they unconsciously obsessed over. Their problems came from *not* thinking about what they were doing, from *not* making conscious well-reasoned decisions.

Do that long enough, McElwee thought, and your life will become so unbearable you'll have to sit down and think.

Okay, so Leanne and I were hard-headed. We had to sink pretty low before we woke up and pulled ourselves together. But we did, each in our own way. It was a hard road, and there was no big prize at the end. No happily ever after, but we did become better people. I have to give us credit for that.

And it hit him then that this was the exorcism he'd been looking for. The answer was not to destroy the past, but to accept it. Accept it and it stops hurting so much. And then you can move on.

He decided he'd submit the story to a literary journal. There was one down in Texas with a circulation of almost four hundred. It had published a number of Mae Chang's stories, including his favorite, "Excursion." They paid fifty bucks a story, and they mailed you five free copies of the magazine that you could pass out to friends.

Fifty bucks would buy a nice dinner. Or better yet, a present for Veronica. Sure, she was a pain in the ass, but that curse she'd put on him had done him good. *I think an author who writes crappy novels should be punished by having to live inside the novel of an even crappier author.* Like rubbing a dog's nose in the mess he made on the carpet. She was absolutely right. He was cured.

On a cold dark afternoon six days before Christmas when the rain and snow were blowing sideways, McElwee drove his old Chevy to the rare bookstore two towns over in search of a little treasure for Veronica. She was a book geek through and through, sniffing the interiors of her favorite literary works and fanning the pages against her cheek.

What did she like?

Pretty much everything. Classic English literature, early twentieth-century Irish. African and Indian works depicting the effects of colonialism. Caribbean historical fiction. Political biography. Erotica. Sci-Fi and Fantasy, but only if they didn't include werewolves.

The rare bookshop, with its stacks of musty hardbacks, was especially dark in the December gloom. The pale old proprietor, with his bald pate and fringe of stringy white hair, sat stooped at the counter. McElwee couldn't tell if he was awake or asleep, alive or dead. The man looked like one of those Halloween haunted-house figures that at first appears to be a statue, and then suddenly springs to life to frighten young children.

"Anything interesting come in lately?" asked McElwee.

The old man turned his head slowly, like an ancient dog waking from a nap.

"Got a first-edition Chandler. *The Big Sleep.* Hardcover. Good condition."

How apropos, thought McElwee. Now there's a detective novel done right. He considered for a moment that it contained many of the same tropes as that stupid dream he'd just lived out in the Turnerverse, and yet it was considered a classic. And deservedly so.

"How much?" asked McElwee.

Much more than the fifty dollars he'd been thinking of spending.

"Ah, what the hell. Let's have a look."

As the old bookseller went to fetch the book, McElwee watched a blonde-haired woman of thirty or so enter the store. She was thin, well dressed in a grey wool skirt and black waistcoat, with perfect posture and a dancer's athletic grace. He watched her pull a book of poetry from the shelves, watched the feelings play across her face as her thoughtful blue eyes scanned the pages.

He hadn't noticed himself walking toward her, drawn as if by magnetic force. And then somehow, he was right beside her. If great literature was a collaboration between writer and reader, a willingness to meet halfway with open hearts and open minds, this was his reader, the one he'd been trying to connect with in every work he'd ever written, the one whose ordinary, everyday world would burst into color at his words. She was the woman from the bedroom at 123 Terra, the one whose willingness to extend compassion had allowed her to be so moved by the painful story of his marriage.

How did she get here? Into this world of flesh and blood? He put his hand on her shoulder, his eyes wide with wonder.

"Dorothy?"

She turned at once, brow knit, eyes narrowed, nostrils flared in anger.

"Excuse me?"

"Um..." McElwee flushed as he realized he'd just accosted a stranger. Her tone showed no trace of Dorothy's gentleness. He had intruded on an intimate moment between a writer and a reader and the reader was understandably upset.

"Excuse me?" she said again. "Do I know you? Or do you just go around putting your hands on women whenever you feel like it?"

"No, I—"

"Am I wearing a sign that says come touch me?"

"Sorry." He backed away. "I was lost in thought."

"Keep your thoughts and your hands to yourself!"

McElwee left the store six hundred dollars poorer, with a first-edition gift for Veronica and a sense of burning shame at his blunder.

In his apartment that night, he buried himself beneath a pile of wool blankets, Tabitha purring on his belly, and thought of Dorothy.

I'll write something immortal for you, he promised. I will! Reach into you and touch the beauty in your gentle heart!

He closed his eyes, keeping the image of her front and center, and repeated to himself, "I will see you in my dreams. We'll be together, soul to soul, and when I wake I'll write a story worthy of your great spirit!"

Then he fell asleep and dreamed he was having sex with Veronica Mayweather, with her natural red hair and her great big boobs and her playful, adventurous enthusiasm. And when he woke in the morning with sweat-soaked sheets and a pounding heart, he couldn't remember a thing about the woman in the rare bookstore or the image of that gentle soul he'd tried to hold in his mind before falling asleep.

His head spun as he stood from the bed. He had to shower, get to the Amtrak station. The New York train would leave at eight.

What time was it now? He checked his phone.

Six thirty-three.

Below the time display, he saw a text from a number he didn't recognize. "Skip the train, Joe. There's a first-class ticket waiting for you at the airport. Limo will pick you up from LaGuardia. See you at lunch."

Who the hell was that?

He called the number. It went to voicemail. "You've reached Purvis Greenback. I can't take your call right now…"

He hung up, opened the browser on his phone, and searched for Purvis Greenback.

Hmm. The CEO of that big media company that had been buying up all the New York publishing houses. Why would *he* be calling?

McElwee was supposed to meet with his editor and agent to negotiate a new publishing contract in the wake of *Extraordinary Joe*'s runaway success. Now the CEO of the whole media conglomerate was sending his personal limo?

Well, well, well, McElwee thought. They're bringing out the big guns for a guy who, six months ago, was Joe Nobody.

Then he read the text from Veronica. "Good luck in NYC. But watch it, Joe. Once you've been bit by the money bug, it's a slippery slope. I've seen it sooooo many times!"

In the shower as he soaped his face, he said aloud, "Why does she always have to be such a downer? She was so much more fun in the Turnerverse."

# 38

"So, what do you think of the new name?"

Purvis Greenback, the CEO of More Media, ate in a hurry and talked with his mouth full. He was a big man, McElwee noted. Eats a lot, and often. I would too if I could afford to dine in a place like this.

After flying McElwee first class to New York, Greenback's personal limo had whisked him to an uptown restaurant fancier than any he had ever seen. The doorman, with his immaculate double-breasted suit, looked like he spent more on dry cleaning than McElwee spent on rent.

"The new name?" McElwee asked.

More Media had just completed its acquisition of the last of the Big Five publishers. On a call with investors, Greenback had told the company's shareholders the move was to secure supply for the company's other media outlets, including its movie studios and streaming platform.

"It's a pure business play," he told them. "Like when that tire company bought up the Brazilian rainforest and turned it into a rubber tree plantation. If you want your business to be secure going forward, you need to lock down long-term supply. We now have virtually every writer in America under contract, and we're running a production line from hardback to paperback to streaming. Boom, boom, boom! We're making bank!"

Joe was still trying to get over his reaction to the buffet. A table thirty feet long, loaded with more food than he could eat in a year. At one end, roast beef, chicken simmered in a rich cream sauce he couldn't identify, oysters on the half shell, lobster tails, shrimp as large as the palm of his hand. At the other end, puddings, cakes, pies, and tarts inlaid with fruits of every color, works of art almost too beautiful to be eaten. And most astonishing of all, everyone here, every diner in this restaurant, could take as much as they wanted!

How long had this world existed? Had these people been living it up all those years he'd been grading papers and eating beans in his wet, gloomy basement?

Why did they seem so unimpressed by this lavish spread? The diners looked as bored as factory workers in the company cafeteria, chatting blandly, not even looking at the great abundance of delights laid out before them.

When he loaded his plate, Joe had looked to his left, then to his right, and then behind him until he was sure that only the man in the white chef suit carving the roast beef was watching. Then he stuffed half a dozen prawns into the pockets of his jacket and thought about how later, in his hotel room perhaps, he could cook up a bowl of shrimp-flavored ramen, toss in the giant prawns, and have it actually taste like shrimp for once.

At the table now, he began to have second thoughts about that plan. My jacket's going to stink, he told himself. I'll have to get it dry cleaned. And how much will that cost?

He had just begun to chastise himself for falling back into the poverty mindset, swiping food from a buffet and fretting over pennies as he'd done for the past twenty years, when the CEO asked him about the new name.

"The new name?" McElwee said.

Was More Media a new name? No, that's right. They'd followed the trend of other media and tech companies and shortened it to a senseless non-word. Morer. And then they added that stupid tag line: Tomorrow, even morerer.

"It's catchy," McElwee said. "Like a step up for 'more.' Like, more than more, if there is such a thing."

"Exactly!" roared Greenback, his ultrawhite teeth gleaming with delight in his flushed red face. He said the word so loudly, McElwee turned to see if anyone was staring at them.

"We hired the best branding house in the business. They're the ones that came up with Sy-Fy. Remember when it was just

The Sci-Fi Channel? Who the hell wants to watch that?" Greenback chuckled and clapped his hand down on McElwee's shoulder.

The good-old-boy grab, thought McElwee. The captain of the football team likes me!

"Yeah, so look, Joe." Greenback spoke through a mouthful of bread and beef. "Let's cut to the chase here, ok?"

"Sure."

"You heard about Niall Turner?"

"Uh, no? What about Turner?"

"The guy's nuts." Greenback twirled his finger next to his temple, giving the universal loco sign as his cheeks bulged with food. "We got him locked up in a mental institution."

"What happened?"

"Attack of conscience. Listen to this." Greenback picked up his napkin and wiped his mouth. McElwee noted that the man barely chewed his food, swallowing whole chunks at a time. He wondered if he suffered from indigestion.

"You know how many books Turner has written so far?" Before McElwee could attempt a count, the CEO answered his own question. "Thirty something in the Howitzer series? Seven Joey Sternjaws? Twenty-nine in that other series, and then the standalones. Comes to almost two hundred titles. Collaborations, mostly, but still... And you know what the average body count in those stories is?"

"Wait," said McElwee. "Does someone actually keep track?"

"Yeah, I got this AI bot to read his entire oeuvre. Took sixteen seconds. Anyway, the answer is a dozen. He kills about twelve people per book. Whores, kids, cops, you name it."

Greenback poked his fork into a prawn on McElwee's plate, stuffed it into his mouth, and said, "And now, you know what? The guy feels guilty about all those people he killed. Can you believe it? And—"

McElwee noted it was a very dramatic *and*, the kind the comes right before the kicker.

"And now he's decided he needs to humanize all those people. He's locked in a mental ward writing with crayons because the place won't let patients have anything sharp. He says, all these people, these characters, I killed them all, and they didn't even have backstories. They were just bodies to be sacrificed on the altar of plot. What kind of god am I?

"You see what I'm saying here? The guy is bonkers. Thinks he's God, sitting there with his crayons in the nuthouse writing backstory for how many characters? Let's say two hundred novels times twelve bodies, that's twenty-four hundred people. Twenty-four hundred backstories! The guy's never gonna finish. You gonna eat that?"

Before McElwee could figure out what *that* meant, Greenback had pulled another prawn from his plate.

"It gets worse," he said, chewing furiously and gulping down chunks. "This crap he's writing, it's not even stuff we can use. It's... it's fucking *literary*!" He said it like it was a dirty word. "He's writing about *feelings*, Joe! The kind *women* have! What the hell am I supposed to do with that? Huh?"

McElwee wasn't sure if he was supposed to answer.

"Which brings me to you!" Greenback's fat hand clamped onto McElwee's shoulder and gave it a firm squeeze. "For decades, Turner was a reliable production line. Cranked out potboilers like clockwork, right into the maw of a hungry readership. The goose that laid the golden eggs, right? Well now he's washed up. We need a replacement. I haven't read *Extraordinary Joe* but I've seen the sales numbers, and let me tell you, Joe, I'm impressed. You knocked it out of the park, and look..."

He leaned in, spoke confidentially in a low voice. "This isn't the kind of thing a big CEO just comes out and says to a lowly writer, but we need help, Joe. Our streaming platform, Bingehose, is starting production on the Joey Sternjaw series. It's got a nice noir feel, you know? Los Angeles, best city in the world! Nineteen forty-eight. Back in the day when men were running the show. None of this politically correct bullshit. It's a throwback, right? Gives people a window into when America was fun. You know, secretaries and bosses drinking and screwing each other, that sort of thing. Sure, there's lots of killing, but it's glamorous killing, not that sordid true crime stuff you see on *Dateline*.

"Anyway, Turner owed us one last installment in the Sternjaw series. Book eight, Sternjaw finally takes down the big crime boss. That nasty Harley guy. Only Turner's nuts now, in the psych ward with his crayons and we can't count on him for anything. You know what the last character he wrote was? Some big dumb Polish thug. Guy was a piano mover and part-time enforcer for Harley's gang. Turner felt bad for him, thought he wasn't fleshed out enough, so he turned him into a concert pianist with dreams and aspirations and a fiancée. I mean, what the hell? Who wants to read about a big dumb Polack diddling a keyboard? Where's the excitement in that?"

Greenback gulped down half a glass of wine, wiped his mouth, and said, "So what's your price, Joe?"

"You want me to write the last Sternjaw book?"

"That's what I'm saying. Name your price and we'll have a deal."

McElwee almost said ten thousand dollars. That would be more than six times the advance on his last literary novel. Then he reminded himself it was time to stop thinking small. You're not poor anymore, Joe. Your last book brought in sixty thousand on the first royalty check and over a hundred and fifty grand on the second. This guy's a billionaire. They think on a whole other level. If you lowball him, he won't take you seriously and you'll just be setting yourself up to be used in the future.

"Half a million," he said.

"Are you fucking crazy?" Greenback was wiping his face again.

"You said to name my price."

"Yeah, well name something reasonable."

"A hundred and fifty thousand."

"How about a hundred? I think we can both agree on that."

"A hundred thousand?" McElwee thought for a moment. "Did Turner leave an outline for book eight? Because I know he writes extensive outlines for all his books and has ghost writers fill in the rest."

"Ah!" Greenback's face lit up. "I was hoping you'd want to see it."

Greenback pulled something from his pocket and laid it on the table with a flourish. McElwee picked it up and stared in bewilderment at the beer-stained paper napkin.

"Other side," said Greenback. "Flip it over."

McElwee turned it over and read the scrawl. One line, five words. "Clever detective catches bad guy?" He looked up at Greenback. "That's the outline?"

"It's a little thin, but it gives you room to work. All you gotta do is wordsmith that. You got your clever detective, you got your bad guy. What's not to like? You put words on paper, we feed it into the Morer marketing juggernaut, sell a few books, and then the big jackpot: the nonreaders sitting in front of the TV. The couch potatoes who passively consume everything we throw at them. We got twenty million Bingehosers on the edge of their seats, waiting to see how the great Sternjaw epic wraps up."

McElwee's heart sank. *This* was what counted as success?

"Why do you look so glum, Joe? This is the easiest assignment in the world. And it'll seal your reputation forever. You won't just be the potential heir to Niall Turner, but the literal heir. The one who wrapped the series!"

McElwee ran some calculations in his head. How much would it cost to make the transition from Styrofoam shrimp ramen cups to fresh giant prawns once and for all? Because once he got used to that lifestyle, there was no going back.

How much would a nice house cost? Not a modest starter house or a fixer-upper, but a home he was proud of? A home that could make him forget all those years in cold drafty basement flats with the clanging radiators that, for all their noise, never managed to warm the place?

He had pulled in over two hundred thousand so far on *Extraordinary Joe*, and he might reasonably pull in another two hundred grand. But even a modest home these days cost over half a million. If you wanted something nice, you had to start at a million, maybe even a million-two.

And what if *Extraordinary Joe* was his only hit? He'd put down all his cash on a house, and if he failed as a writer and had to go back to teaching, he wouldn't earn enough to cover the mortgage.

And what about a car? The old Chevy had been on life support for years. It wasn't going to take him much further.

And what about retirement? He was forty-three years old and might live another forty-three years. On what?

Even if he stayed in his damp basement, saved the whole two hundred thousand and went on living frugally, the money would run out.

Greenback's eyes lit up. "I can see you're warming to the idea, Joe! Tell me what you're thinking. How do you see this Sternjaw series wrapping up?"

"I see a femme fatale."

"I love it!" said Greenback. "Big tits?"

"Excuse me?"

"How big are her tits?"

"Who cares? It's a book."

"Uh-uh." Greenback shook his head. "You gotta think ahead to streaming. What kinda tits are these people gonna see on Bingehose? 'Cause I already know who I want to cast. Tata Zakimbo."

"The porn star?"

Greenback gulped down the rest of his wine and motioned to the waiter for more. "Yeah, she wants to go mainstream."

"She's a redhead, right?"

"Born and bred. With curves like Jessica Rabbit." Greenback's hands traced an hourglass figure in the air above the table. "And she'll do her own sex scenes. Means we don't have to pay for a stunt double. Saves us money." He tapped his temple and winked. "You gotta think like a businessman here, ten steps ahead of the game. Every dollar I don't have to pay to staff goes into my own pocket."

"Wait, what does she sound like when she speaks?"

"Tata?"

"Yeah."

"I don't know, I usually watch her on mute. Why?"

"Because the character I have in mind here is very sharp. Perceptive, insightful, and articulate."

Greenback looked confused and Joe wasn't sure, but the man's frown may have indicated a trace of annoyance. "Why would you want to put brains into a woman with tits like that?"

"She's actually one of the most interesting characters in the book."

Now Greenback was clearly annoyed. "Joe! We're talking thriller here. Male fantasy, capiche? Our audience lives vicariously through Joey Sternjaw, the average Joe they can identify with, but he's living a larger than average life. Right? Sticks it to the bad guys, sticks it to the ladies, just like these shlubs fantasize about but don't ever get to do. We're aiming at the thirteen-year-old boy inside of every middle-aged man. You give this femme fatale a brain, and she's gonna start nagging."

"Exactly," said Joe. "She's Sternjaw's conscience. She keeps him true. Doesn't let him get away with any crap."

Greenback shook his head and frowned. "Joe, that's a wife you're describing. I know, I've been through six of them! These guys, the Bingehosers, they already have wives. That's what they want to get away from. They don't want responsibility. They want fantasy. They want to be the guy who shoots Boss Harley and then falls into bed with Tata Zakimbo."

"I was thinking of having the female lead kill Boss Harley."

"Why? No, wait. I know! It keeps the women engaged. Am I right? Show a tough girl in action, give the ladies something to fantasize about too."

"That's not really what I was thinking, but—"

"Ok, what else?"

"We start out with Joey Sternjaw being framed."

"Yeah?"

"He wakes up in an empty apartment with a bloody knife in his hand. There's a pile of stolen cash and jewels beside him on the floor."

"God!" cried Greenback, smacking his forehead. "What the hell happened? Where'd the jewels come from? Whose are they? Whose blood is on the knife?"

"He doesn't know."

"He doesn't know? Christ, Joe, you got me on the edge of my seat already. Then what?"

McElwee tapped his temple. "The rest is all in here."

"Really? You wrote the whole thing that fast?"

"I could write that book in my sleep," said McElwee. And then he thought, actually, I did. I was unconscious the whole time I was in the Turnerverse. My brain spun up the story after Veronica put her curse on me.

"Tell me how it ends!" Greenback cried.

"Frump."

"What? No!" The CEO was flabbergasted. "The loyal sidekick? But why?"

"He was having an affair with Lady Astor."

"My God! How do you writers come up with this stuff?"

Easy, thought Joe. Just bash your brains out, collect the debris, and call it a thriller.

"Not gonna tell me, huh?" said Greenback. "That's fine. Trade secrets, right? Here, sign this." He slid a sheaf of papers onto the table.

"What's that?"

"A contract."

"What's it say?" Joe squinted at the text.

"What do you mean, what's it say? It says you give us words and we give you money. Just sign it already."

"Wait, where's my agent?"

"I got rid of her. What do you need her for? To skim fifteen percent off the top? I'll tell you something, Joe. A little bit of business advice. First thing you do is get rid of the middleman. Or is it middle woman? I can never tell, you know? It's like we used to say actor and actress, but now actresses are actors too because we're not supposed to call out their gender. Or is it sex? I don't know. But then some chick flies to the moon or runs for president and all of a sudden it *is* important that she's a woman. Well, which is it? Are we supposed to call out their gender or not? Why can't women make up their minds? Sign that, Joe." He stabbed his fat finger against the dotted line.

"What am I agreeing to?"

"Why's everyone so hung up on details? I told you. You give us words, we give you money. And the only words I need right now are your first and last name, on that line right there." He tapped the line again to remind McElwee where to sign.

"This will give me the hundred thousand for book eight of the Sternjaw series?"

"And more," said Greenback with an encouraging grin.

"All right."

As soon as McElwee signed, Greenback nodded toward a man at the neighboring table. The man stood, whisked the contract from beneath McElwee's pen, and left the room.

"Wait," said McElwee. "What did I just sign?" He had a sinking feeling.

"Don't worry," said Greenback, swirling his wine. "You don't have to worry about anything anymore."

"Somehow that doesn't reassure me."

"You're a Morer boy now!"

"Boy?"

"No more worrying about rent."

"Because I'm finally going to buy a house," said McElwee.

"Won't have to worry about a mortgage either," Greenback added cheerfully.

"Because I'll buy it outright! Cash up front!"

"No utilities."

"Well, I still have to pay those."

Greenback shook his head. "We take care of that."

"Really?"

"You'll have your very own room in our writers' colony."

"Writer's colony?"

"It's in Burbank, Joe. We bought the old city jail on foreclosure."

"Wait a minute—"

"A window in every cell. You'll get an hour in the yard in the morning, and an hour in the evening. Same as the other writers."

"Sorry, what?"

"We follow the Geneva convention to the letter, Joe. To the letter!" He thumped the table to emphasize those last three words.

"Wait a minute," said McElwee. "Back up here. What did I just sign?"

"All past and future contents of your mind belong to Morer."

"Surely that's not legal."

"You made it legal when you signed. Don't worry, Joe. We're paying you."

"How much? No amount could possibly be enough for—"

"God, will you writers stop with the whining? What is *with* you people? First you complain that no one reads your work and you're starving, then someone comes along, puts you in front of an audience of millions, showers you with cash, and you complain about *that*."

"How much money?" Joe asked.

"I don't know." Greenback swilled down half a glass of Chardonnay in a single gulp. "It's a complex formula involving square roots, the natural logarithm of pi, and a lot of negative numbers. Don't try to understand it, Joe. We got it from the record industry."

"But the record industry was infamous for not paying their artists!"

"So, what? Now you want special treatment?"

"I want to know how much I'll get paid."

"You'll know when the check arrives. We print the number right on the front. And we spell it out in words too. For you writers."

Greenback nodded toward two men at another table. They rose, took McElwee by the arms, and dragged him kicking and screaming toward the exit.

"Wait!" he cried. "You can't do this!"

Greenback smiled broadly and said, "Contract, Joe."

"But I need to pack!" McElwee said. "I need to get my clothes! And Tabitha!"

"Youze'll get cloze at da writin' colony," said the larger of his two escorts, a rough-looking man in a broad-shouldered suit. "Company cloze, like da resta da writers wear."

"Why are you talking like that?" Joe cried. "You can't do this to me! I'm an artist! This isn't how it works!"

He was almost to the door when he noticed the sly little smile of the woman at the corner table, the woman with the shock of black frizz, the thin nose and big owl eyes.

"Wait!" said McElwee, shot through with sudden doubt. "*Is* this how it works?"

He read the bookstore owner's lips clear as day as she mouthed the silent words. "Waking up now, are we?"

# THE INSPIRATION FOR THIS BOOK

On July 6, 2022, there was a discussion on Hacker News about Ronald Knox's *Ten Commandments of Detective Fiction*. Knox was a mystery writer in the early twentieth century who laid down some ground rules for the detective genre that most writers agreed made sense.

In the Hacker News discussion*, some readers complained about writers who violated these rules. User hirundo posted the following comment which directly inspired this book:

> Detective fiction is usually about the process of justice when someone breaks a commandment, frequently the sixth, often involving seven, eight and nine. I'm looking forward to the meta-detective novel in which a critic investigates violations of the Ten Commandments of Detective Fiction.
>
> The appropriate punishment might be more suitable to a fantasy novel: To sentence the writer to live for a time as a character in a world built by an even more arbitrary, capricious and inscrutable author than Jehovah.
>
> I'd read that.

I found the idea so compelling, I sat down and wrote *The Sellout* to make fun not only of those who violate the commandments, but also of the tropes and excesses of the detective-thriller genre in general, which happens to be a genre I love.

* https://news.ycombinator.com/item?id=31999508

# ALSO BY ANDREW DIAMOND

# IMPALA

After four years on the straight and narrow, Russell Fitzpatrick has a boring job, the wrong woman, and an itch for something more. All he needs to get his life going again is a nudge in the wrong direction.

When he receives a cryptic email from a legendary and slightly deranged fellow hacker—his old friend, Charlie, whom he knows to be dead—he tries to tell himself it's none of his concern. But the guy who stalks him across town at night, the two thugs waiting in the alley, and a ruthless FBI agent let him know his days are numbered if he doesn't turn over the money Charlie stole.

The problem is, Russ doesn't have it. As his enemies close in from all sides, Russ slowly unwinds the mystery of his old friend's paranoid mind and finds that Charlie left behind something worth much more than the money. And no one but him is on to it…

Winner of numerous awards, including:

- The Writer's Digest Gold Medal for Genre Fiction
- The Readers' Favorite Gold Medal for Mystery
- A best of the year nod from IndieReader
- An Amazon.com Editor's pick for one of the best mystery/thriller titles of September, 2016

"[Diamond] gets all the little things right, as well as the big ones, in this riveting novel…A convincing, complex cyberthriller". – Kirkus Reviews

"A fast-paced, page-turning, relentless story from start to finish." – IndieReader.com

"A smart, wholly engrossing cyber crime novel… Impala is full of hard-hitting insights that ring true.." – BestThrillers.com

"A compelling, unexpected mystery that's hard to put down and satisfyingly complex to the end." – D. Donovan, Senior Reviewer, Midwest Book Review

# GATE 76

Freddy Ferguson #1

A mysterious woman fleeing an unknown terror boards the wrong plane at San Francisco International and disappears into the heart of the country. Freddy Ferguson, a troubled detective with a violent past, believes she's the last living witness to a crime that has captivated the nation.

Sifting through the wreckage of her past, he begins to understand who she's running from, and why. Now he must track her down before her pursuers can silence her for good.

A modern crime thriller with elements of Raymond Chandler and the classic pulp novels of the 1950s, this character study wrapped in a tale of crime and redemption was named to Kirkus Reviews' Best Books of 2018.

"A consummate thriller with some of the best characterization you'll see all year." – Kirkus Reviews (starred review)

"One of the year's best thrillers." – BestThrillers.com

"A phenomenal mystery novel with dynamic characters and a gripping and intricate plot." – Susan Sewell, Readers' Favorite

# KILL ROMEO

## Freddy Ferguson #2

Not since he saw a woman hurry off a jetliner shortly before it exploded in midair (*Gate 76*) has detective and former boxer Freddy Ferguson faced such a deadly puzzle as when he comes across the body of a well-dressed young woman, nameless and unidentifiable, deep in the woods of rural Virginia. In her room at the town inn, she left two mysterious notes hinting at a love gone wrong.

The trail to her killer leads through organized crime, espionage, and the international race for technological supremacy to a seemingly unremarkable man the FBI and CIA have been trying for years to pin down.

"Ferguson is deeply relatable thanks to Diamond's elaboration of his inner life, which matches the intrigue of the murder mystery at the heart of the story." – The BookLife Prize

"To say Andrew Diamond knows how to spin a thriller of a story is an understatement. Add this to your summer 'must read' list!" – Feathered Quill Book Reviews

"The murder mystery driving *Kill Romeo* is first-rate. So too is the writing… The sum is a novel that is simultaneously entertaining, suspenseful and cathartic." – BestThrillers.com

# 32 MINUTES

### Freddy Ferguson #3

A corporate executive vanishes without a trace. His domineering boss wants him back in the office, ASAP.

Did Karl Larsson run off with a mistress? Was he kidnapped? Or had he just walked out once and for all on a life of debt and struggle?

The deeper Freddy Ferguson digs into this one, the less it makes sense. The statements from Larsson's long-suffering wife, from the stoner security guard who was the last to see the man alive, and from the respected reporter known for having the inside scoop just don't add up.

Where is the truth in this most perplexing of cases? Maybe in a slip of the tongue by an arrogant man, or in a dopesick junkie's account of a seemingly random attack. Maybe in the pocket of a man who stalks without fear of being seen, or in the multimillion-dollar transactions of an anonymous shell company.

One thing's for sure, Freddie needs to crack this case before he becomes its next victim.

"Diamond crafts an absorbing plot and surprises with well-placed curveballs that will have you guessing what's coming next with each page turn. But the well-fleshed-out characters are the highlight of the book." –Pikasho Deka, Readers' Favorite

"Thoroughly absorbing and completely unpredictable." – D. Donovan, Sr. Reviewer, Midwest Book Review

"Brace yourself for an action-packed, emotional ending." – BestThrillers.com

# THE FRIDAY CAGE

Claire Chastain #1

Someone new has taken an interest in Claire Chastain. He circles her house when she's alone and follows her on errands across town. He tours her home while she's away, leaving little things disturbingly out of place. He may even be involved in the recent death of her childhood friend.

But who is he? And what does he want?

Claire soon discovers that, like Cary Grant in *North by Northwest*, she's caught up in someone else's dark conspiracy, and she has no choice but to play the game. The only exit from her troubles will be the one she makes, if she's smart enough to figure out when and how to make it.

"Fast-paced and exciting… ingenious and gloriously unpredictable…. one of the most compelling and odd private investigators in literature today." – Jack Magnus, Readers' Favorite

"Claire Chastain may be Diamond's deepest protagonist yet. Anxiety, fear, grief, regret and the quest for survival and justice are constantly simmering under the surface… A deeply psychological crime thriller that perfectly captures the terrors of both murder and life itself. Highly recommended." – BestThrillers.com

""Psychological growth and confrontations test Claire's many abilities to survive and lead her to question her inclination to run away from some hard truths… Diamond's ability to weave the greater mystery into her personal failings, shame, and self-examination process contribute to a believable character whose struggles are moving and action-packed. Readers who enjoy solid thrillers spiced with psychological depth and revelation will find *The Friday Cage* a compelling saga…"–Diane Donovan, Senior Reviewer, Midwest Book Review

# THE REISMAN CASE

Claire Chastain #2

A wealthy business owner asks investigator Claire Chastain to solve a simple case. Is his employee stealing or not?

From the moment she's hired, subtle clues tell her something's wrong: the unbusinesslike business owner, the lingering scent of a woman on the stairs, the rustle in the curtains where someone watches from above.

Claire's gut tells her the case isn't about theft. Her investigation turns up a pathologically anxious suspect, a deeply dysfunctional family, and a murder that she herself appears to have committed.

"If I had known what this case would turn into," she reflects, "I never would have accepted it. No one walks into a burning house."

But she's in it, and she has to find her way out…

"A gripping murder mystery… Claire, is a forceful and tenacious character. Even though the exterior of her personality is rough, she is genuine and relatable. The storyline moves at a steady pace, with the suspense and intensity growing with every page." – Susan Sewell, Readers' Favorite (5 stars)

"Diamond, who writes well-acclaimed crime, mystery, and noir fiction, is here exploring for the second time the mind and motivations of Claire Chastain, a daring, highly intelligent female who has her own secrets to repress… The twisted tale causes her to cross paths with some dark characters and dodge life-threatening peril, while maintaining a certain enviable inner strength and outer cool." – The Feathered Quill

# WAKE UP, WANDA WILEY

Hannah Sharpe has been written out of all eighteen of Wanda Wiley's romance novels. A runaway heroine who won't conform to the plots laid out for her, Hannah has been consigned to a realm of fog deep in the recesses of the author's imagination.

Trevor Dunwoody, the protagonist of a macho action-thriller that Wanda has regrettably agreed to ghostwrite, is single-minded and obtuse, understanding only what he can beat up, shoot, or screw. Like Hannah, he's a character Wanda doesn't know what to do with. When he appears one day in Hannah's fog world, she can't convince him he's in the wrong story.

Hannah knows she'll be stuck in the limbo of Wanda's subconscious until the writer can find a suitable story to cast her in. But Wanda, trapped in a disastrous relationship with the philandering narcissist Dirk Jaworski, is sinking into a deep depression. The pot she smokes to self-medicate impairs her ability to write and thickens the fog of Hannah's timeless isolation.

As Hannah explains her predicament to the thick-headed Trevor, she begins to realize that she knows her author better than her author knows herself. If she can only break out of the limbo of Wanda's subconscious and nudge the writer in the right direction, she can free them both.

But how can Hannah penetrate the fog of her creator's mind from within? The answer is right in front of her in the form of the big, dumb, action-ready tool, Trevor Dunwoody.

"Diamond's prose is funny and barbed, particularly the dialogue between Hannah and Trevor. He takes aim at genre conventions and their unrealistic treatment of characters… Clever and surprisingly compelling. A well-crafted literary satire with something to say about genre fiction." – Kirkus Reviews

"A bright and original rom-com with a cast of really enjoyable characters… Hannah's exploits in the subconscious of her creator are sharp and extremely witty." – K.C. Finn / Readers' Favorite

# WARREN LANE

Susan Moore is about to hire the wrong man to investigate her philandering husband, Will. There's something not quite right about that detective, but he's all she has at the moment.

"Warren Lane" drinks too much and has a hard time staying out of trouble. He's just the kind of guy Will's mistress can't resist. And everyone is starting to figure out that Will is hiding a lot more than his affair with a reckless young woman.

"A quirky, intriguing and wholly original read." – Readers' Favorite

"The more I read, the more I fell in love with the book. At some parts of the book I laughed so hard I almost cried." – Margaret Yelton / Goodreads

"A wonderful, suspenseful, romantic, and fun read! Andrew Diamond writes a story rich in emotionally drawn characters that grabbed me from the beginning and literally pulled me right into the book." – Debbi DuBose / Goodreads

"There's enough of the crime noir element in this touching comedy of errors to give it and the characters realistic complexity and depth… This would make a fantastic screenplay." – Wanda / Goodreads

"Totally enjoyed this contemporary comedy of errors. I read a lot yet few are as memorable as this fun book. Andrew Diamond should be on best-seller lists. If you haven't read this yet, treat yourself." – The Illustrated Home Librarian

# TO HELL WITH JOHNNY MANIC

John Manis, aka Johnny Manic—charming, stylish, impulsive, and reckless—is racked with guilt over the secret he doesn't dare tell. Marilyn Dupree, passionate and volatile, has too much money and the wrong husband. Johnny and Marilyn have a chemistry like nitrogen and glycerin, and that makes Detective Lou Eisenfall very uneasy.

"Poor Lou," Johnny muses as his mind begins to unravel. "There's a madman running around his town, and who knows what he'll do next."

This riveting tale of deception, murder, and psychological suspense was named one of the best of 2019 by BestThrillers.com.

"A feverishly readable psychological noir." – Kirkus Reviews

"A truly riveting tale of deception, murder and psychological suspense… One of the year's best thrillers." – BestThrillers.com

"Diamond cultivates an engrossingly dark vision of a protagonist whose alter ego takes over in many different ways. The build-up of psychological suspense and the evolution of evil is truly compelling… highly recommended for crime readers who like their stories introspective, brooding, and psychologically astute." – D. Donovan, Senior Reviewer, Midwest Book Review

# ABOUT THE AUTHOR

Andrew Diamond writes mystery, crime, noir, and an occasional comedy. His books feature cinematic prose, strong characterization, twisting plots, and dark humor. Amazon editors named *Impala* a best of the month mystery, and IndieReader named it to their best of 2016 list. *Impala* also won the Readers' Favorite Gold Medal for mystery and the 24th Annual Writer's Digest award for genre fiction.

*Gate 76* was named to Kirkus Reviews' Best Books of 2018, while BestThrillers.com selected both *Gate 76* (2018) and *To Hell with Johnny Manic* (2019) to their best of the year list.

You can follow Andrew on Amazon, Goodreads, and on his blog at https://adiamond.me.